T0082780

WARRIOR LIFE

WARRIOR LIFE
THE RISE OF A LEGEND

ROHAN "G-MONEY" GOLDING

WARRIOR LIFE
THE RISE OF A LEGEND

Copyright © 2021 Rohan "G-Money" Golding.

All rights reserved. No part of this book may be used or reproduced by any means, graphic, electronic, or mechanical, including photocopying, recording, taping or by any information storage retrieval system without the written permission of the author except in the case of brief quotations embodied in critical articles and reviews.

This is a work of fiction. All of the characters, names, incidents, organizations, and dialogue in this novel are either the products of the author's imagination or are used fictitiously.

iUniverse books may be ordered through booksellers or by contacting:

iUniverse
1663 Liberty Drive
Bloomington, IN 47403
www.iuniverse.com
844-349-9409

Because of the dynamic nature of the Internet, any web addresses or links contained in this book may have changed since publication and may no longer be valid. The views expressed in this work are solely those of the author and do not necessarily reflect the views of the publisher, and the publisher hereby disclaims any responsibility for them.

Any people depicted in stock imagery provided by Getty Images are models, and such images are being used for illustrative purposes only.
Certain stock imagery © Getty Images.

ISBN: 978-1-6632-2251-0 (sc)
ISBN: 978-1-6632-2260-2 (e)

Library of Congress Control Number: 2021909263

Print information available on the last page.

iUniverse rev. date: 05/05/2021

CONTENTS

INTRODUCTION

ONE HUNDRED THOUSAND LEAGUES UNDER THE SEA

G-Money was putting a new spin on the popular ghetto term *pimpin'*, making history he could never report, in fact, as the first G to pimp at twenty thousand leagues under the sea. He'd pimped out his submarine to look like a literal replica of his favorite movie from childhood. Growing up in the gutter, he'd always dreamed of the sea, not just of having a place on the beach either; he wanted an island one day. Now, he not only had his own isle, but here he sat in his very own submarine. Pimpin' …

He believed he was the first fugitive from the law to ever stay on the run this deeply underground, so to speak. In the past ten years, he'd only been to the surface a handful of times. With the NSA hunting him as the world's most wanted terrorist, technology had made it harder and harder to stay hidden in the traditional ways that his predecessor Mutulu Shakur had. Satellites in space chased him now. He shook his head and cracked up as he looked at his latest printout of reported sightings of him around the globe. He'd used those same technological advances against them, sending look-alikes who'd already had a similar facial profile and, thanks to top-notch plastic surgeons, had perfect a face that would fool a satellite image from anywhere in the world.

"G-Money's been sighted in Tokyo, Japan! Scramble the embassy marines!"

"Notify the CIA station in Hamburg, Germany—we've got him!"

He loved watching the chases that were broadcast live, around the globe, on cable television's hottest news networks and listening to the anchors talking in multiple languages. Sometimes, he turned them all up at once and got one of his bitches to polish him up while he watched CNN, Fox News, BBC, Al Jazeera, and Afro Worldview. He didn't stage too many fake sightings in Africa; he needed too many countries on the continent to piss off the big dogs. G-Money was the most famous fugitive in Africa and was welcomed into jungle villages like a god. He always brought truckloads of cash with him but didn't hand it to the general in charge of the territory (although he got his cut too); he handed fistfuls of thousand-dollar bills straight to the people, just like Pac had prophesied in *Thug Life*. It bought him a loyalty from the streets that was priceless. He'd done it in all the hoods around America too, and with the advent of YouTube, cell phone videos of G-Money handing out millions of dollars to the people had racked up a staggering billion views over the past ten years. The governments that chased him hated it, as they watched him buy the love of the public they were counting on to turn him in, for a joke of a small reward.

G-Money had always beaten the age-old reward-for-snitching model by simply outbidding his pursuers. He wasn't buying loyalty; he was rewarding silence, and it hadn't failed him yet. Any time he was in danger from legitimate snitches ratting him out, he simply had them killed. He could get to anyone at any time—he'd discovered that police in foreign countries were easy to bribe and prison guards were even easier; he had armies of inmates in prisons around the world. He'd invested in the infrastructure of all the major prison gangs as soon as he'd gone on the run, using his first generation of loyal plants in the Bloods and Crips to run money to the books of all the shot-callers, and it had filtered down from there. If there was a bribe to be made to a warden or captain of the guards or even someone on the local cell-block level, G-Money financed it from behind the scenes.

He'd almost eliminated prison rape from the incarceration culture in the process and even had been able to work into the bribes, which he paid monthly to the prisons around the United States, unofficial conjugal visitations for hundreds of inmates of importance. G-Money knew pussy was a more valuable commodity in prison than even drugs, and he'd been rewarded with a rock-solid army of prisoners around the world—some he'd even broken out or arranged early parole decades before they were due to be released. He had the added bonus of watching local law enforcement jurisdictions, state police budgets, and tens of millions in federal fugitive-hunting resources be eaten up in trying to recapture his soldiers. So far, they were 0 and 1,134, according to *America's Most Wanted*, which had even given G-Money and Warrior Life their own month of weekly Friday night specials. John Walsh had cemented G-Money's legend as the head of Warrior Life, especially after G-Money surprised Walsh by phoning in live on the air from an encrypted sat phone. He'd spent twenty minutes on the line with John Walsh, making him the most famous journalist in the world to ever interview a living fugitive. Shit, his ratings had been bigger than the OJ Simpson verdict that night, and it drove law enforcement crazy.

He cracked up every time he thought about how much money those fools were wasting deploying their best resources—both in men and machinery—to capture G-Money, only to discover, when they ran the DNA, that it was a look-alike. *Suckers!* He'd pulled this off over one hundred times in one hundred different locations around the globe over the past ten years, costing his pursuers over $100 million in wasted resources. Of course, the US had footed the bill for the manhunt, essentially paying the budgets for foreign spy services all over the world by reimbursing millions of lost dollars in failed apprehensions, based on the false identifications alone, not to mention his master network of planted snitches. G-Money had used their same technology to set up a ghost satellite system around the world by giving safe haven to the world's most wanted hackers. G-Money had them all in his pocket and, most important, under his protection. He loaned them out occasionally to some of the dictator governments that he occasionally did business with on the black market. They always paid handsomely in cryptocurrency or new state-of-the-art equipment, and he always made sure everyone got a cut.

All of his hackers were multimillionaires—his lieutenants—and even the dictatorships that had risked foreign invasion by aiding him had grown richer by their association. In turn, he got access to their satellites, where his hackers controlled a competing satellite in space, allowing his network to infiltrate the back doors of all the major spy satellites, from the US to their main allies in Europe and the Pacific Rim. He had access to their intel on everything from his Warrior Life network's activities to the moves that those hunting him were planning to make against him. He always stayed several steps ahead; it gave him room to dance on those bitches! He was the Keyser Söze of the shit; Frank White bending them bitches over and spanking them raw!

G-Money looked out at the exotic colors of the fish swimming around him. He loved it down here; it was like living in a dream, and he was living the dream! He had the finest women in the world living with him on this very submarine—all expertly trained, all loyal to the death. He'd saved many of them from that fate in the first place or from lives in sexual slavery as part of the human trafficking network. Everyone who lived under G-Money's protection had it in their best interests to protect him. It was a brilliant strategy that inspired a loyalty, and that hadn't betrayed him yet. He loved to pump the Jan Hammer *Miami Vice* theme into the Magico M5 sound system that he had throughout his sub, especially during orgies with his bitches. G-Money—living the dream; if only everyone could go on the run this way.

He would have his weekly secure satellite conference with his top lieutenants around the world in an hour, and he always made sure he had a solid three- or four-hour orgy before those tense sessions. The saying was true: "Heavy is the head that wears the Kangol" (G-Money's version of a crown). G-Money even sold his own personally designed Warrior Life Kangol and a website of other G-Money and Warrior Life merchandise, which he gave away by the wardrobe to his crew. Soon after the Black Lives Matter movement protests were internationally televised, right alongside Tupac and Thug Life apparel and signs, the entire world saw the grassroots strength of the Warrior Life movement on the backs of hoodies and on signature sneakers and boots, belts, jeans, T-shirts, and even tattoos and ladies' black-satin panties. G-Money didn't wear diamonds, but he gave them away to his people in the streets. He always was dressed in his trademark black during the video conferences; it commanded respect. Although everyone answered to *him*, he had to have answers for everybody, every time.

G-Money had studied all the masters of wartime leadership and strategy, from Niccolò Machiavelli's *The Prince*, to *The Art of War* by Sun Tzu, to, of course, his teacher Tupac Shakur. Now, G-Money was passing on his own message, creed, culture, and code to millions of young Warrior Life soldiers in training around the world. They wore his logo proudly in their everyday fashions, flashed his Warrior Life sign—a clever hybrid of the Bloods' and Crips' gang signs—and even used his own form of Warrior Life cryptocurrency that had been the hottest to trade on the black market for years now. G-Money had it all, but he had everything to lose if a single order was carried out with even a slight error, so he kept close and current counsel with his leadership team every week. Anyone who missed the call was presumed captured or killed, but so far, no one had ever missed a call, even those incarcerated, courtesy of G-Money's network's mastery of smuggling specially encrypted smartphones into the prisons around the world, where they were running their own units.

Today's call had a special focus—a daring mission for which he wouldn't need volunteers but would have to select someone who wouldn't want the job. Someone who was getting lazy; someone he intended to flush out on the call to test his loyalty, to see who he really was working for and, if necessary, have him killed in front of everybody, right there, live, on the call.

G-Money had an army of assassins, loyal to him and him alone, planted in every one of his units around the world. They were silent in their status—until activated—often not even known as killers among the group but rather posing in the easier-to-miss positions of computer technicians, something that let them move around anywhere with complete freedom and without suspicion. He relied on them to plant bugs or hidden cameras, when needed, in bedrooms or control centers; to plant viruses on computers; or to silently monitor email traffic for anything remotely resembling traitorous talk. It was not lost on G-Money that many in his ranks were ambitious; all were wanted, and if someone didn't feel he was moving up fast enough, he might try to betray G-Money. It hadn't happened yet, but today might change everything.

G-Money couldn't afford to look weak; he had to strike like a cobra if his instincts and intel were right. He couldn't turn over anyone in his movement to law enforcement, which made it that much easier to kill them—and justifiably, for breaking the first rule of his feared yet followed G-Code. He relished making the rare example out of a subordinate who forgot who was running this shit, and today, he almost hoped he was right so he could spank this bitch out in the open.

G-Money's Warrior Life Council—WLC—was made up of about as colorful a cast of criminals and characters as the world would *never* see, sitting around a table together. They didn't even exist, as far as the world's top intelligence services were concerned. They were merely a rumor in the mill, word on the street, a myth in the mist, a tree falling in the forest.

G-Money had designed them to be completely invisible and to control the underworld. His council was made up of the following:

OG *Cobra* ran the West Coast Crips from underground and was now on the FBI's Ten Most Wanted list, right next to G-Money, for blowing up the LAPD's Intelligence Division, killing one hundred cops and earning him godlike status in every West Coast hood, where, even after he went on the run, he still controlled a roving network of encrypted smartphones.

OG *Daco* was tech-boss of Warrior Life's underground IT Nerve Center. He ran the world's top team of hackers, who—rather than work for the CIA or NSA equivalents in every corner of the civilized world, and to avoid prison—sought shelter on the dark web, from which Daco recruited. At present count, he controlled two hundred of the world's most talented hackers, all corrupted by the nature of everything that had made them hackers in the first place. Daco now used their skills to control his massive online robbery operation of the slush funds of the governments that wanted these very hackers. It was genius; the governments couldn't report the thefts because the money was dirty to begin with, in most cases, and everybody got a cut. Other hackers were experts in ghost satellite hacking, allowing G-Money to move spy satellites away from his organization's safe spots around the globe. They created online identities for fictitious snitches that fed false leads to law enforcement from points all over the globe about G-Money sightings or alleged safe houses for Warrior Life fugitives, which turned out to be convents of nuns or Muslim mosques during prayer. He cracked up, watching SWAT and fugitive-apprehension units, in full gear, storm a temple full of terrified praying Muslims. The riots were always leaked to the media, as each failed attempt to capture G-Money and his crew only heightened their urban legend.

Kashmir and Mikel were Daco's right- and left-hand programmers and chief hackers. Both were killed in the first year of G-Money's life on the run, and he'd responded similar to the wrath of the Russians in the 2016 US elections, shutting down entire city electric grids, sewer systems, traffic lights, transit systems, cell towers—everything that made not only cities but, more importantly, their law enforcement apparatuses run. For good measure, he'd left the lights off for a week during a summer in New York, causing the worst riot in the hoods in the city's history, and pulled the same disciplinary measures in LA, causing the worst riots since the Rodney

King verdict in the early '60s. Of course, the gangs ran the looting crews, others ran the protests, and G-Money T-shirts, hats, and hoodies became the rage of the rebellion. G-Money avenged his team's death by running law enforcement ragged with riots that they couldn't stop or even contain, let alone control. It looked like chaos, but behind it all, G-Money quietly controlled the strings, pushed the buttons, called the shots, and became a legend.

OG Ganja was the most wanted drug lord in the world; he ran Jamaica's drug trade and answered only to G-Money. Thousands of dealers across eighty countries and four continents answered to him, directly or indirectly, kicking up better than 50 percent wholesale of anything they made on the street. Anyone who held out on the WLC ran out of product; it was that simple.

OG Dollaz was the minister of the Warrior Life crew, in charge of bribes. He could pay off anyone in cryptocurrency, and he managed all the online holdings of Warrior Life's corrupt career, from law enforcement to politicians to civic and religious leaders, prison wardens, captains of the guard, military officials in different countries around the world—anyone who needed to keep the wheels turning got their palms greased—period—and so handsomely that G-Money hadn't been betrayed yet. There hadn't been one prosecution of any corrupt official in ten years, even though many had tried. Witnesses never talked; they just disappeared. Their evidence did too. G-Money had bailiffs, court clerks, and evidence-room custodians all on Dollaz's payroll. Dollaz had estimated their annual bribe budget at 25 percent of Warrior Life's annual take, but it was well worth every penny. Freedom was expensive, and everyone had been proven corruptible. Everyone had a price, a vice that needed to be fed, from drugs to gambling to even charities that G-Money quietly funded from behind the scenes with illicit profits, which made him a folk hero to millions of peasant villages around Africa and the islands and to hoods in every major metropolitan area, from across the US to Europe, from Japan to Russia and China. Dollaz ran it all on the WLC's own cryptocurrency, which was now the most valuable bribe money in the world.

Solja Sasha had been G-Money's personal bodyguard for the past decade, recruiting a secret circle of *soljas* who guarded G-Money with their lives, most of whom he'd bought out of sexual slavery. It was the touchstone throughout every loyalty G-Money inspired, for whatever his soljas owed him, he'd paid a far greater price than they could ever reimburse him, in terms of avoiding a life of sexual slavery, passed around from man to man and country to country. G-Money freed his women, and they were loyal to him forever. Fortunately, he had a special taste for those trained in the military or martial arts—preferably, both—and whatever skills, knowledge, or expertise they were missing, he taught them once they were part of his ranks.

G-Money had two hundred female bodyguards stationed all over the globe, from his islands to his submarine, and everywhere in between; many were mothers to his seventy children around the world. G-Money raised most of his children via Facetime and royal visits, where they felt special even to have him there, for all the attention the local islanders and security forces paid their father, but G-Money was a good father. He felt proud he had relationships with all seventy-one of his children, ranging in ages from under a year to over eleven years old. He planned to take each of them aboard his master submarine as they became teenagers and begin training them in the ways of Warrior Life. It was here that G-Money would pass on his ways, like the Jedi, which would last long after he was gone; his ways would live on. His customs would pass from generation to generation, and while outsiders joked about the number of offspring he'd produced in a decade, from Africa to Harlem, he knew his time was short and his knowledge long. Just as Louis Farrakhan with his thirteen children or Martin Luther King Jr. with his eight children, some illegitimate, or Malcolm X or Jesse Jackson, G-Money was arguably the greatest modern civil rights leader of his generation, and his tribe would live forever, based on the creed and seed he was spreading now.

CHAPTER 1

LITTLE GS

G-Money loved turning weak girls into strong women. His baby-mamas were all strong, all taught in the ways of Warrior Life, and all raising their children side by side, without jealousy or other petty concerns. Their eyes were on the big picture, the bigger mission, and G-Money was head of the commission. His biggest challenge had been what to name all his children. Their mothers wouldn't dare offer suggestions unless asked, but he laughed when he thought of George Foreman naming his sons George II, George III, George IV. He couldn't exactly name them all G-Money, so he started thinking in terms of his legacy; he decided to keep the G in front of every one of his sons' names. G—and the rest he left to his soljas. G-Money trained and trusted his women well, all except one.

Breaking his heart this day was the alleged traitor in his council, one of his closest original bitches, Solja Sista. He'd pulled Sista out of a whorehouse in Africa, gotten her off heroine, turned her life around, and allowed her to give birth to his firstborn son from the diamond armies, and how had she repaid him? By betraying him to the tune of $4 million in Warrior Life cryptocurrency. Sadly, she'd fallen for a simple trap set by one of his hackers who ran the WL financial networks on the dark web. Today, she would realize just how far she'd gone over the edge when her own son stepped up to behead her on national Warrior Life television.

Sadly, reminiscent of the movie *Running Man*, G-Money's executions had become some of the highest-rated television and replayed videos on YouTube and the other networks that Warrior Life had infiltrated. People sent the videos around in email chains and made dupes, like the *Faces of*

Death movies, buying him a trillion dollars in loyalty that he could never pay for. Although a son killing his own mother might seem savage, it could never be as savage as her betrayal had been.

Everyone in Warrior Life was rich. All that was required was loyalty; then freedom and wealth beyond their wildest dreams was guaranteed for life. G-Money's rules were simple: never betray him; never betray the Warrior Life. Death was the only punishment; it sent the only message— that he needed to be respected at all costs. G-Money had to hold every one of his soljas to such a standard, or it all would come within an inch of unraveling. The tension in a string was tighter than anything of longer length because if a traitor got an inch, better believe they'd take a mile before you even realized they were off the reservation. G-Money had decapitated traitors on live television to his Warrior Life network, which had the bandwidth of a major cable network in the ghost satellite world. It arguably was the most watched YouTube feed of any independent movement. Black Lives Matter? Not once Warrior Life came on the scene. Warrior Life co-opted their movement with a real message and—more important—a real solution. Those soljas loyal to Warrior Life could eat and their kids slept in warm beds at night. They brought their entire families out of poverty. Warrior Life offered every benefit a community could dream of. All G-Money commanded in return was loyalty; for disloyalty, the punishment was death—period.

Warrior Life even had its own weapons, designed by the finest weapon-makers in the world. Many would have been in bankruptcy, if not for the invisible capital infusions that Warrior Life had made to their basic bottom lines. G-Money was silently a major shareholder in major government weapons contracts from the US to Europe, from Russia to China, and he got a heads-up on all the latest technologies, from drones to missiles, machine guns to handguns, knives to the finest Samurai swords on the collectors' market.

G-Money's firstborn son, G-Pac, would guillotine the traitor tonight with one such sword, and his demonstration of loyalty would behead any notion of betraying him again. He'd spent the previous week with his boy; he spent one week a year with every boy or set of siblings—fifty sons and twenty-one daughters—and spoke by Facetime to each of them every week. He prided himself on being a father to all his children, and today would be no different, as they showed what true loyalty to Warrior Life meant to them. The single strike of a blade would silence any doubt that G-Money ran this shit worldwide.

With the betting world watching, Warrior Life cryptocurrency was trading at the highest values yet, as G-Money watched a stock market he controlled with the simple utterance of the words "Thug Life, bitch!"—code for *kill*. G-Money channeled his mentor Pac at any time he could echo his words in new action, and it had become a crowd chant that he watched on satellite feeds across twenty TVs, which ran across one of his sub's walls, from every one of his controlled territories, where the beheading would soon be broadcast out into the cyber world, embedded in Twitter feeds and Facebook messages, texts, emails, and every other form of social media that could be infiltrated.

He watched the crowds chanting from around the world, chanting for blood, like Romans in the Colosseum; and, like Caesar, he gave the order, and his eleven-year-old son, G-Pac, swung the sword down on the traitor's head. The crowds were silent for a moment, in shock, watching a son behead his own mother, watching justice in a world where it was rarely witnessed, yet thrilling his army with a pride they could only take in righteous retribution. A traitor to one was a traitor to all; one act of betrayal could bring down the whole show. Imagine if G-Money's now-headless traitor actually had pulled off the theft. She'd have had to wash the money somewhere, which would have exposed the dark web to spotlights and scrutiny. Maybe they'd even gotten hold of her before Warrior Life had. It was G-Pac who had caught her in the act and first acted on the Warrior Life code he'd been taught since he could first walk, and he knocked out his own mother before she could complete the illicit transaction.

Boy kings were nothing new in Africa or Roman times, and with G-Money's fifty sons ranging in age from babies to eleven years old, he was grooming successors as he raised his boys. He needed just a few more years on the run to raise them into manhood so that if he ever was caught or killed, they could take over; his movement's newly minted prince, G-Pac, was now in the running. Soon, son would join father on his master submarine, learning the ways of Warrior Life and how to be a leader. He would one day have all his boys under his wing, one-on-one, but the first would be his firstborn son. He'd raised the boy by video on Facetime, seen him countless times throughout his first decade of life, and celebrated every birthday, but he had held him in his arms only once, at birth, and then had disappeared into the night. This would be the first time he would hug G-Pac, and it reminded him of another reason why Sista needed to die; she nearly had robbed him of raising his son.

Nobody fucked with G-Money and lived to brag about it. He'd have her body fed to the sharks, but her head would sit on a shelf, with other enemies he'd collected over the last ten years, in a special closet of his private chamber. He had the heads of former dictators—of countries he now controlled behind the scenes—everyone who had ever opposed or betrayed him, and now he would have to make room for Sista Solja. With one slice, he had beheaded the latest snake in his garden, but G-Money was always on guard. He had to live that way, but it was his edge that kept him on top. He was a chess player, and he had just checkmated the world.

CHAPTER 2

CHECKMATE

G-Money sat on the top of his submarine, watching the sunrise cascade across the open ocean. Not a cop for ten thousand miles. Not a drone in the sky. He raised his bottle of Cristal in a toast to all the fallen Warrior Life soldiers. For a moment, he flashed back fifteen years to the Iraqi desert, drinking a bottle of 110-degree water in weather of the same temperature. He'd come a long way. Back when G-Money first enlisted in the US Army, he'd done so to escape the streets, not because he was afraid but because he was wanted by a local drug lord, whose girl he'd been tapping on the side. Another fond flashback interrupted his reflection momentarily, but G-Money soon returned to the desert background, camels, Humvees, explosions, and definitely no oceans. He'd been stationed along the Iran border, and had been given the worst field duty a soldier could ask for: helping guard the heroin trade between the Iraq and Iran territorial tribal leaders that kept peace in the region.

It had been a terrible education to give any unhappy soldier, and when G-Money had his "psychological breakdown," as the military termed it, or his epiphany, as it was when he was reborn as one with his immortal leader Tupac Shakur, he was caught right in the middle of a crossfire that broke out between young guns from two rival tribes, battling for territory. Bullets whizzed by his head like in the movies, except this was real life. G-Money was using dual fields of vision between his infrared night-vision goggles and their reverse-view cameras that gave him eyes in the back of his head so he could nail punk bitches from both sides of the border. He'd crouched on one knee once the gunfire started, not to pray but to give him a better field of sight, while everyone else stood firing at each other. Going back to his street days, growing up in Brooklyn's Bed-Stuy war zone, he followed Scarface's move in the nightclub of aiming for the kneecaps. He took down a field of fire on each side, and suddenly, there was silence. Total silence in the desert night.

The stars overhead lit up the outlines of the dead bodies lying around him. Only G-Money had survived the gunfight. His entire combat squad was dead, killed by the terrorists, while his bullets had ripped holes through the knees and then chests and heads of ten men. His heart was racing like a train as he rumbled to his feet, snapped on his silencer as he reloaded, and fired an extra shot into the foreheads of each of his ten victims to mark them. He called in the excursion on his encrypted phone, and since the US Army wasn't intended to be there in the first place, spy satellites immediately erased the feed of the entire battle. The only evidence was G-Money's secret video feed that he'd imbedded into the infrared on his weapons and helmet, transmitted to a trusted solja—one of his first—back at a lonesome military satellite base, manned by one person at a time in the desert, somewhere in Utah.

He'd quickly downloaded the feed on a ghost network and saved three digital copies, which then were emailed to three separate encrypted email accounts that G-Money had already set up in case something like this happened, and he needed to cover his ass. Finally, he deleted the feed by oral code word just in time, just as the US Humvees pulled up to retrieve bodies.

They had expected to find him among his fallen comrades. They seemed surprised to find him alive, not because they questioned his skill as a soldier but because they'd expected him to walk into the ambush along with the rest of his squad. No one would have found out, since they didn't exist on paper anyway, and the war would have taken a new turn, with the terrorists making it over into Iraq and giving the president's authorization, which he'd needed to extend the US occupation there.

G-Money should have died that day, and from the two bullets he took, he nearly did. He'd certainly played dead for the US hit squad that the CIA had sent to make sure no one from his squad survived. Using training they'd ironically taught his combat platoon—to stop their heartbeats for sustained seconds by holding their breath; then exhaling and kick-starting it—G-Money did just that when they'd picked up his limp body and thrown it on top of the pile of fallen comrades on the back of the Humvee.

"He's dead," an anonymous soldier had told his superior.

G-Money remembered staring up at the stars, waiting for his moment to roll off the pile and into the void. They didn't discover he was missing for another one hundred miles, and by then, he had made his way to a village he'd protected for months. The village medic gave him medical aid and then shelter for a month while the bullet wounds—thankfully, both through and through—to his torso and right leg healed. That bullet had missed his manhood by half an inch, thank God.

Back home, on paper, the ten terrorists he'd killed had earned him a Purple Heart and a Medal of Valor, awarded posthumously to his family. G-Money had made his way back across the borders along the same drug-smuggling routes he'd protected for months, making new contacts at every stop, where his military intel and expertise about the trail helped ferry him along with a pharmacy of good times, all the way up through South America, where G-Money had been recruiting soljas into Warrior Life's earliest ranks.

He'd been forced to kill more than a few loud-mouthed bitches who thought they ran shit until G-Money had run right over them and taken control of their territory in the process. By the time he got back to Brooklyn and killed off the top drug lords on some Batman shit in the middle of the night, leaving their bodies in the streets, with the Warrior Life logo branded on their foreheads, his "WL" became one of the most popular new tattoos on the streets and in prisons around the world.

When he'd assumed the identity of Greg, his alter ego, he'd started a war with McNair and the NYPD, setting them up to think they'd taken down G-Money after beating him within an inch of his life. When he woke up, strapped to a hospital bed in a psych ward, his fingerprints had been cleverly replaced with the identity Greg would be interrogated under. Thanks to his CIA-sponsored military training, he was Jason Bourne when they pumped every truth-telling drug they could into him, from quetiapine fumarate (400 mg, one tablet, twice a day), to prazosin HCL (2 mg, one tablet at bedtime), to trazodone HCL (50 mg, one tablet at bedtime), among other colorful pills and long needles—the typical psychological torture cocktail. G-Money had played his role to a T, acting out psychotic episodes and spilling the story he'd preprogrammed into his mind, which sent his interrogators down the rabbit hole and deeply into cyberspace, fictional hacker networks, and names of ghost organizations that didn't exist but that his hacker contact had set up in advance of his capture.

His army identity was still deceased. If he ever needed the trump card of his recordings of the illegal excursion on the Iraq/Iran border, he'd use it, but setting Greg up to become G-Money gave him a ghost identity that McNair and his army of government bounty hunters would be chasing forever. They were chasing a ghost, and the day he escaped from the psych ward, the legend of G-Money had been born, and that chase had begun.

Watching his past through the bubbles in his Cristal bottle, G-Money laughed so hard that he almost spilled his fine wine down the side of the submarine. He toasted a whale who had surfaced and then dived again into the Indian Ocean, where G-Money was presently floating, and he shared a final moment with the sunlight he wouldn't see again for months—a small price to pay for his freedom—as he relived scene after scene of his cinematic escape from McNair and those sick doctors' clutches.

It had started with the plant he'd had in the room—the nurse who was one of his Sista Soljas, who'd injected—among the countless needles of shit being pumped into his body—a counter-agent that made his entire psychological breakdown an act. The second and last shot she gave him had launched him into a rehearsed seizure and initiated an emergency evac to a more proper hospital after a bomb threat had simultaneously been called into the ER of the hospital where he'd been held. Rushed to the roof under the guard of two MPs and his loyal nurse—who'd knocked both guards out cold with simultaneous injections in the neck of a powerful, instantaneous sedative—the rest of the cavalry had broken through the door to the roof and made it on to the helipad just as G-Money cut the throat of the pilot and threw him down into their arms, with his middle finger in the air, yelling *"Warrior life, bitches!"* His Sista Solja piloted the medical chopper to safety a few buildings away, where they'd switched choppers and been out over the sea before the powers that be could organize any kind of pursuit.

He'd landed on a hijacked aircraft carrier over the Atlantic in international waters before stepping foot onto this very submarine for the first time. Bought on the black market in trade for some of the drug traffic he controlled on Warrior Life's newly established dark web network,

G-Money's next move would make him the world's most wanted terrorist and begin a ten-year manhunt that continued to this very day. Because they'd been able to take his blood at the hospital while he was lashed to the torture bed, a DNA match had emerged in the Sudan, in a village where G-Money's first son had been born while he was making his way back to the States, after the initial illegal Iraq/Iran border slaughter that had started this war. When he received word at the bottom of the sea that a drone had bombed the village, along with his first solja wife and son, into oblivion—under the CIA claim of its being a terrorist camp—he'd uploaded the video of the illegal CIA slaughter of his fellow comrades to the web, and it had gone viral.

Congressional hearings had followed; the first CIA officers ever charged with war crimes in the history of the agency and several high-ranking generals across several branches of the military had fallen very publicly in the crossfire, making G-Money the number-one target of their hit squads, from the US Navy SEALs to the Special Forces, from the Marines to the air force's best pilots. All were ordered to gun for G-Money on a revenge mission that was officially sanctioned by the White House. Warrior Life grew as he fought back, building the biggest underground army ever to exist in the process.

His hacking force rivaled the combined best minds of every country that was hunting him. G-Money had used their power to help swing presidential elections in multiple countries and had raided the slush funds of those same greedy leaders to make them broke overnight. Soon, the dominos fell. G-Money controlled the heads of seven dictatorships, puppet governments that protected his interests in exchange for being puppet leaders. It was a plush life, but he reminded all of them to always remember: they each were only a president for life, and the term limits were ones G-Money could lay down any time his hit squad was green-lit. He knew that hit squads were hunting him all over the world at the same time—some men, some machines, some in the air, some on the ground, some underwater at this very moment.

G-Money had phantom subs swimming all over the world on the bottom of oceans, all empty, carrying decoy signals—essentially underwater drones—and with the latest state-of-the-art holographic technology that made it appear to radar and satellites overhead that they were carrying full crews. In a few cases, these decoys had even been torpedoed on the off chance they were part of the Warrior Life fleet. G-Money hadn't lost one of his real subs yet. His own swam oceans so deep that the best satellites in the world couldn't detect it. He'd seen worlds that the rest of the world above him hadn't yet. He'd recorded it all; he had archives that would make Jacques Cousteau jealous, another asset for the Warrior Life library.

Presently, he was busy overseeing the construction of Warrior Life's first fully functional underwater base. His hackers had pulled the plans from a Russian cyber-safe, where they'd hidden their latest blueprints for the future. It was well below any space or sea satellite's radar capabilities of detection, and anyone within the bunker could survive a nuclear blast on the surface of the earth. His children would grow up with the most beautiful sea creatures, from sharks to eels, octopuses to exotic deep-sea fish, and he would watch his sons grow to men, if the dream came true. He was still a couple of years from finishing construction, stress tests, missile silos, electromagnetic impulses, and amphibious hologram technology that made the structure invisible from even fifty yards out or more. The military of any major country would kill for this sort of shelter. Now, as he felt his royal sub dive, he said goodbye to the last of the sunlight, and began making plans for his next big coup.

CHAPTER 3

OPERATION LIBERATION

THE WORLD HAD MANY ILLEGAL trades sold on the legal markets in industrialized countries: furs, high-end endangered wildlife trafficking, oil smuggling, cigarette trafficking, human trafficking (arguably its most disgusting trade), and its most lucrative, the diamond trade. Even waste disposal, or environmental cleanup, as the Mafia in the US called it, was booming, with more and more multinational corporations dumping their chemical waste off the coasts of third-world countries.

G-Money had a piece of it all. He controlled an invisible empire that spanned from Africa to South America, the Middle East to the Pacific Rim. That also meant he had multiple agencies hunting him at any given time, requiring a sophisticated bribery system, paid for entirely in Warrior Life cryptocurrency, which meant he had to keep the currency chasers off his back at the same time. G-Money paid a high price for his freedom; then again, anything beat a prison cell back in the States, five hundred feet underground in the highest-security military prison in the world. If G-Money had to live below the earth's surface, he preferred it to be in his luxury submarine.

This morning, his business concerned a diamond mine in Sierra Leone, Africa, which Warrior Life controlled after saving a local warlord from an internal revolt from a faction of his younger, hungrier soldiers. General Kony had become famous in 2012 when a video went viral—to the tune of seventy-five million views—showing him making slaves of female children, as young as nine or ten, in the mines and recruiting and putting machine guns in the hands of their brothers at the same age, making rapists of them by twelve, and rampaging across Uganda and Sierra Leone, pillaging the diamond trails, legal and illegal, and costing the existing syndicates billions, worldwide. G-Money had seen an opportunity and had sent his African army of Warrior Life soldiers, based in the neighboring Congo and from the capital of Nairobi. He'd sanctioned the whole invasion legally, as a freedom operation.

It was covered worldwide on cable news—children were liberated, and Kony was decapitated by one of G-Money's Warrior Life generals, live on social media. When General Barca—rumored to be a blood descendant of one of Africa's most celebrated generals, Hannibal Barca of 247 BC—yelled "Warrior Life" on live international television before beheading Kony, it became an invaluable rallying cry and recruiting tool in the six years that followed, as G-Money brought order to an illegal trade once thought to be as uncontrollable as drugs.

G-Money trafficked *only* in marijuana, the highest grades from all over the world, all trafficked freely along his diamond routes, centered in the Congo, and run north through South Sudan and Sudan into Egypt and then the Middle East, where he had a booming clientele among the prince networks in Saudi Arabia.

While cocaine or heroin addiction would get a royal prince removed from the line of succession before he ever took the throne, marijuana was a tolerated Western influence. Because of its decriminalization worldwide, it was now making Warrior Life billions of dollars a year in raw growth and transport, once the product changed hands in the Middle East, Europe via G-Money's network in Morocco into Spain, and through South America and into the United States, where he had calmed competition from the Mexico growers by making them partners. G-Money had brought the murder rates down by 20 percent in every country he dealt in. It was enough political capital to buy him the appropriate government bureaucrats in every Western country he needed to bribe his way into. With the money he paid out, he bought access into their satellite systems via his hacking networks, working underwater around the clock to put every other industry with which he had partnered illegally in better working order.

Any outlaw factions were immediately crushed from within or by G-Money's feared Warrior Life hit squads—he had recruited the most highly trained assassins who had been betrayed, sold out, or left behind by their own governments when it was politically inconvenient. In most cases, G-Money had saved these men's and women's lives, and, in turn, he had earned their loyalty for life. They killed whoever he sent them to kill in the same desensitized way their governments had trained them, only this time, they had a safe home base to return to and the best equipment, intel, and infrastructure support the world over, thanks to Warrior Life's international military connections and officials, owned within every major government in the industrialized world and third-world countries. He paid them handsomely for each flawlessly executed mission, which always was the outcome.

G-Money's Warrior Life hit squad currently employed five hundred of the world's top trained killers, seventy on the Most Wanted Lists of seventy governments around the globe; four hundred dead in combat, as far as those same governments were concerned; and thirty who didn't even exist on paper. These were all female Warrior Life soljas who lived with G-Money on his mother sub. Twenty of them were mothers to children being raised on this very vessel.

If G-Money was ever killed or captured, he could be rescued safely from any country on earth, and his movement would carry on through his children, who would one day run different facets of his vast empire from the ground. He knew he'd eventually have to say goodbye to these sons and daughters, and so he enjoyed every day of being a father to his children.

His love of children on this particular day had him especially incensed as G-Money Facetimed with his top African general in charge of the Congo diamond mines. The general had requested this high-priority meeting to let G-Money know about a rogue general who called himself Guerrilla, a country over, with a nasty methamphetamine addiction that he'd riddled throughout his ragtag army. The army had been ravaging the coastal country of Gabon, next door, for a month now, unleashed like a wild animal as the country struggled to replace its recently deceased dictator. Seeing an opportunity to take control of the territory, G-Money had to quell this rebellion fast, as it was threatening the ports he relied on to export billions of dollars a month in products all over the commerce map, heading to all parts of the world, where the products couldn't be smuggled through traditional borders.

Coordinating the attack from his command center aboard his master sub and looking around at the city of blinking lights, radar screens, live satellite feeds, and drones—G-Money had a fleet of fifty drones patrolling skies around the world at any one time—and coordinating with General Barca on the ground, he had three thousand Warrior Life troops ready to raid from high ground whenever the order was given. This provided G-Money with the on-the-ground intel that OG Kashmir and OG Mikel were feeding to their recently stolen Switchblade drones, armed with the world's most state-of-the-art mini-missiles, designed to micro-target a motherfucker or his village, with instant obliteration on contact. Weighing only five pounds but packing enough explosive to level a city block, G-Money had six on deck this fine morning to hit every strategic stronghold the rogue general had overtaken and rid his little clique's drug problem once and for all in the process, by wiping it out entirely.

Daco turned to G-Money with the same adrenaline-inspired smile he'd seen on every one of his best killers just before their next finest moment of victory on the battlefield. G-Money nodded, giving Daco the green light to paint his latest masterpiece. From space, the canvas of jungle Africa would soon be a blank one. He targeted no innocents but warned everyone who saw G-Money's missiles rain down from the heavens that God was indeed real and watching every move they made. "Watching them and watching over them"; that was what his troops on the ground always told their soldiers and the civilians who didn't want to get involved. They warned his Warrior Life network of any trouble before intel even picked it up, sometimes on official channels, because with bringing order to networks like the illegal diamond mine trades, G-Money had also brought peace and profit to millions of peasants around the globe.

G-Money made it rain money. Those who hadn't yet been baptized with its freedom would hear of the wealth—from their neighboring countries' cousins, even as a rumor, by word-of-mouth, or on social media—that loyalty to Warrior Life brought, directly or indirectly, to every community in which it operated. Today's little demonstration would only reinforce that reality.

G-Money's peace-keeping force was decked out in all the appropriate-looking gear and uniforms and had currency to pay for anything. With General Barca about to get a new promotion to the boss of Gabon's diamond mines, he would bring freedom to the peasant slave trades and be recognized as the new unofficial leader of the country. He'd coordinate the port operations with existing personnel, whose operation G-Money personally supervised, leaving Barca to keep the country's approximately 70 percent of unincorporated villages and territories in line. He'd be embraced like a hero.

With the threat of more mini-missiles falling from God's skies overhead, he had almost a 100 percent guarantee of resistance, even from the existing powers that be. With Barca's signal from the ground, G-Money launched hell on the competition, and within ten seconds, General Guerrilla was retired from the battlefield. He watched from his control center as the world's major cable networks quickly switched to live satellite feeds, coming in from body cams on the freedom force that Barca led as they headed, in real time, into Operation Liberation, as G-Money had dubbed it a month before, when planning for the operation began in principle.

As Warrior Life spread to another impoverished community, G-Money took a call from the President Zuma of South Africa, one of his oldest allies—and one of his first bribes after he'd gone on the run and needed refuge to rebuild. He'd kept a seaside retreat there for decades, protected like an armed fortress under the official guise of a presidential palace, but its soldiers and servants were all highly trained Warrior Life clan. G-Money assured Zuma that no more civil wars would afflict that region of the country, as long as Zuma agreed, along with confirmation that $20 million in new Warrior Life currency had been deposited in his account in Zurich, that he'd recognize General Barca as the new official leader of the country within the next couple months, once displays of order and rapid improvement of local villagers were broadcast to the world, EU, UN, and, of course, the appropriate aid organizations.

G-Money had been privately responsible for a quarter of their new funding in the past decade, so along with the press, who were, ironically, the cheapest graft on his payroll, he also had 15 percent of the private equity in all new experimental drugs hitting the markets in the industrialized world, after they'd heroically debuted throughout Africa, curing and slowing diseases that had plagued the continent mysteriously for decades.

They would unveil their latest discovery, 100 percent owned and developed by Warrior Life in their research facilities at the University of Nairobi in Kenya. G-Money sent thousands of African kids to universities each year on 100 percent scholarships to study every manner of subject matter; arguably, the most lucrative studies were in the biotech and medical fields, and he had a patent on every cure his people uncovered. The universities all got a nice fat cut, along with the governments of those countries, as they then handled the legal exports to foreign territories and pharmacy markets around the globe, but half of all the revenues generated made their way back into Warrior Life's coffers. The remaining 25 percent was given away to the plagued communities that could otherwise never afford them, and in the past ten years, Africa had become one of the most progressive health-aid hotbeds in the world. Diarrheal diseases alone had killed over sixty million people just three years earlier, but that number was down by 70 percent with the cure that G-Money had dropped from the sky, like missiles, via his drone fleet onto thousands of infected villages around the continent. For old-school bitches like malaria, he'd cut deaths from thirty million to fifteen million in the same time. G-Money's R&R budget had exploded in the past two years to 18 percent of Warrior Life's overall budget, but it was worth every penny in both profit and publicity.

He would follow up his devastating obliteration of the rogue general and the thousands of addicted villagers left in his wake with a cure for their methamphetamine addiction, which would soon replace methadone in the States. First, G-Money needed to make sure the media was in place; then he would introduce ibudilast, or MN-166, as it was called in clinical trials funded by Warrior Life, through the cutting-edge new research and testing facilities in Biological and Physical Sciences at the University of Nairobi in Kenya. G-Money had the top scientists in the world on his payroll, and after watching every great gangster movie of his and every generation, he pulled a page from Don Corleone's playbook by investing outside the predicable rackets in which most mobsters had a hand, with an eye on the future. Today's hottest casinos were the laboratories; the blackjack tables were the new polished black countertops and test tubes where the newest experimental drugs were developed, and he made billions in both commerce and political capital.

G-Money liked being on the cutting edge of products no one had thought of yet; that kept him ahead of the competition and his hunters. Think if he'd been in prison for the past ten years instead of freeing so many people from poverty, disease, and sexual and financial slavery in so many countries where they'd have otherwise remained prisoners forever. His freedom was a bell of liberty that rang daily for millions.

He watched as another operation was executed with the kind of precision and perfection that would have made the military's greatest generals—from Hannibal to Caesar to Patton to Powell—proud. One day, G-Money would be counted among those generals, and his pedigree as a leader was one he hoped would be inspiring to everyone under his direction, from his children to his own generals in the field and to the future that would follow him. G-Money was a living legend who made perhaps his most revered personal general, Tupac Shakur, proud every day of his life. With the ecstasy of victory in his eyes, G-Money suddenly felt the glow of the room become infectious. He caught the eyes and then grabbed the hands of two of his baby-mamas and bodyguards and retreated to his private quarters to make love in front of the most gorgeous fish in the world.

CHAPTER 4

OPERATION BREAKOUT

O RLANDO ANDERSON HAD LONG BEEN acknowledged, by both the gangs and guards, as the shooter of Tupac Shakur, and gang life had taken his own years before G-Money had been in the position to avenge it. He could avenge Pac's early passing now through the jailbreak he was about to pull to free Suge Knight from the LA County Jail. After watching Knight languish in third-world conditions for years while awaiting trial for a self-defense case he would never win, G-Money had decided to act for Pac, who, in the same position of power, surely would have bought or fought for Suge's freedom, especially given he was dying anyway. Suge wasn't a saint; he'd been shot on three separate occasions over the past twenty years, starting with the bullet from Anderson's gun that had grazed his head on the night Pac was killed, and then when he'd been shot in the leg at the Kanye West MTV Awards party in 2007, and then six times in the stomach at Chris Brown's VMA party. It was time for Suge to live out his retirement on the coast of Africa somewhere.

G-Money would film the escape with the body cams that his Warrior Life soldiers would be wearing on their LAPD SWAT uniforms as they stormed the jail in response to a "terrorist incident" call, which would put everything in lockdown. Daco had volunteered to be the architect of the prison break, plans some idiot had put online and that he'd updated with inmates smuggled into the state-of-the-art wing for high-profile inmates, where Suge was held. In a nod to the usually incompetent LAPD, they'd actually outsourced the design to private prison architects, who knew their business. Thankfully, Daco's hacker network knew them better, and as of

8:50 that morning—the morning when Suge was scheduled to be sentenced on his recent conviction for first-degree murder, in what the hood widely agreed was a textbook self-defense case—G-Money had all the authority he was looking for to strike.

He would hit them from the underground, using the very plans El Chapo's network had used to smuggle him out of his maximum-security cell in Mexico a few years back. This time, G-Money would take advantage of LA's century-old network of sewer systems and underground tunnels from previous incarnations of the same system, which had simply been papered over too many times to ever truly explore. G-Money had financed the cleanup of LA's notorious Skid Row, getting over one hundred thousand people out of poverty and off harder drugs in what was once termed an urban jungle, using the same model he'd employed throughout the jungles of Africa. In exchange for employing one of the hundreds of acres of legal marijuana-harvesting farms he owned, G-Money had also bought millions of dollars in free information on the architecture of the lost city of tunnels.

Warrior Life had been exploring, cataloging, and outfitting them for months, now with a brand-new lighting system that rivaled any modern drug cartel tunnel across the border. In the process, they had begun building the infrastructure for his eventual US Warrior Life invasion. His test-smuggle through this system—which featured the latest state-of-the-art hover-rail system that was powered completely off the grid and could carry a man of even Suge's considerable weight, as well as the small team of Warrior Life assassins who would help ferry him to freedom— got off the ground without the slightest noise being audible to law enforcement. That far under the city, it wouldn't matter anyway, and as he cleared out every other living pulse, from the homeless to even the rats, Suge's escape route on this glorious morning looked as clear as the radar's dream.

Daco, arguably as loyal a Pac disciple as G-Money, had volunteered to supervise the operation personally. It was perhaps his finest hacking stroke; he looked to G-Money for the OK and subsequently pushed the buttons that would be responsible for the most famous hack of any prison system's allegedly impenetrable security system in California history. G-Money knew the capital that came with Daco's legend, which was growing on the dark web. Once he had Suge safely smuggled out of the jail, city, state, and, ultimately, country forever, he could claim a victory for Warrior Life.

Among its criminal elements, given Suge's own legend, it would make them *the* hippest worldwide gang repping Pac. G-Money wasn't so foolish, not for even one moment, as to think he didn't owe his entire position to Pac. Suge wouldn't be either, as soon as he was freed. Suge had freed Pac, so it was G-Money's honor to return the favor.

A medic was on standby, given that Suge was suffering complications from his multiple shootings, including blood clots, having an appendectomy, and glaucoma; in his fifties, those complications had become life-threatening. G-Money hoped to make the view just a little brighter in his golden years. He asked Daco to pull up the courtroom feed; he had his own private Court TV network, thanks to the bug-sized drone cameras OG Daco had planted throughout the courtroom. The live feed on cable news stations across the world showed the grinning face of a corrupt judge, who had presided over Suge's trial like it was a campaign commercial for his upcoming gubernatorial run. G-Money was about to put an end to the judge's political ambitions by making him the laughingstock of the California legal community. With the verdict set to be read at 9:30 a.m. sharp, Warrior Life prepared to hijack the court proceedings.

It started with a virus that had been planted months ago in the city jail's closed-circuit TV security systems, including the two cameras that ran twenty-four hours in Suge's cell. Now, timed brilliantly at G-Money's strategic direction, to coincide with the rolling blackouts that had plagued the valley all summer—for at least the first hour, until they discovered Knight was missing, Daco, with the simple stroke of a few buttons, blacked out the entire city block that encompassed the LA city jail in seconds. Simultaneously, before anyone knew what hit them, G-Money's demolitions expert, OG Demo, lit his fuses underneath Suge's cell, and suddenly, the floor caved in under a sharply dressed Knight, who had been awaiting his guards' arrival to take him to court. Earlier having been resigned to his fate, Suge's mood suddenly brightened with the short-term blast that knocked the floor out from under him—and then knocked him out cold.

G-Money's force, dressed as LA SWAT, covered the hallways outside the cell, filming it all, like a hundred-million-dollar James Cameron Hollywood action movie. Simultaneously, the targeted explosion took out the left side of Suge's cell as he lay on his bunk, sending everyone, in rehearsed shock, back on their asses for the sixty seconds necessary to physically extract Suge.

Thankfully, all 360 pounds of the unconscious Knight landed safely in the arms of his liberators, as his hovercraft glided through the dark tunnels of LA's underground, in true Warrior Life fashion, to freedom.

Handed off within three beautifully executed minutes to the waiting VSV—for which G-Money had financed the prototype and which *Popular Mechanics* recently had reported as "normally associated with Navy Special Forces or racing, so this is the first time we have seen a narco-sub which uses this design, semi-submersibles ... and designed to be faster than other semi-submersible designs"—Suge was speeding off the coast of Tijuana into international waters by the time he regained consciousness. A trademark cigar awaited him in the outstretched hands of two of G-Money's finest Solja Sistas, who'd volunteered to participate in the rescue mission and were now riding him as his boat rode over choppy waves to smooth freedom.

Suge laughed and looked skyward as one of G-Money's Sistas whispered updates into his ear. He saluted his cigar to the sky, knowing Pac and his liberator were watching. After filming the whole escape in real time, G-Money would leak the footage to the news networks within a couple of hours, making that much more of a laughingstock of the same bitches who had beaten G-Money within an inch of his life, a decade earlier. As a magical finishing touch, he had scored the escape to Pac's anthemic "How Do You Want It?," giving Suge the royal send-off he deserved as he left the coast he'd changed forever.

Warrior Life naturally would claim responsibility for their latest liberation, and while editorials raged online and on air, with the usual debate over whether they were a network of terrorists or freedom fighters, G-Money felt the perfect *adios* would come with Pac flipping the middle finger to the camera while he exhaled a heavy hit of California's finest, and a "Sponsored by Warrior Life" logo was the last shot before the video blacked out. In an effort to keep pace with the second-by-second-coverage speed that cable news networks were expected to broadcast, they switched immediately back to the stunned face of the courtroom judge, who had just finished watching the same slap in the face to his honor that the world had just seen. As the realization that his political future had disappeared in an instant, along with his defendant, he seemed to lose his mind, perhaps feeling an overdose of judicial authority that erupted as he beat his gavel into the bench. He broke his wrist in the process and subsequently threw the gavel wildly toward the courtroom camera, in what would be his final act as a California court judge. It hit a bailiff, nearly blinding him, and a mini-riot soon erupted in the courtroom, sending a fever of chaos out into the streets. The people responded with a block party that spanned the city of Compton and no doubt reverberated all the way upstairs to Pac, partying in heaven.

CHAPTER 5

OPERATION G-SWEEP

ALL AFTERNOON, G-MONEY MONITORED THE mayhem that consumed LA like a wildfire, earning condemnations from even the US Attorney General and the president himself. *Fuck Trump!* For months, stickers had been papered on the bumpers of White House and Trump-era government employees; it was one of Warrior Life's favorite political pranks to date. Today's bumper sticker—sponsored by the WL and tagged on the bottom right corner of all the latest WL paraphernalia that swept the hoods on a day off—would honor one of America's greatest racists, Christopher Columbus. Hundreds of packets had shown up at church gyms and basements, community centers, homeless shelters, and grade school gyms the day before, stuffed with hundreds of hundred-dollar bills, alongside the face of his other biggest rival in the LA hoods at the moment, G-Currency. G-Money was doing for his people today!

Every one of the custodians, from preachers to gym teachers, knew better than to steal a single yard from these young'uns, as they each received anonymous donations on the morning of the stickering of $100,000 per outlet—from church to charity—for their own operating budgets, to simply encourage the youth of their communities to express their First Amendment right to free speech and expression in the form of protest. Today's bumper-sticker message would make an enemy of the people of a certain charlatan who had been trying to infiltrate G-Money's stronghold on the inner city in recent months, a newly released con artist from the California prison system who had spent five years studying G-Money's doctrines and tried to co-opt them for his own gain with the clever *Warrior Reformer* banner.

Known on the inside as G-Currency, he had plagiarized G-Money's moves in small doses to build a little crew inside the prison system. Ironically, half of Warrior Life plants had reported every theft to G-Money directly. Today, G-Currency's own soldiers would kill him, and he would be made an example of in the streets in a rare show of gangster power in modern US culture. G-Currency was also about to become one of the most famous rats of his time, a move that only helped G-Money as he directed the manhunt away from his network and onto his rival's, giving the US authorities the kind of small fry that they could make look like a main course for the media—statistically, they struggled to even understand their own crime stats anymore, with the way Warrior Life had altered them.

The series of bank robberies that G-Money was coordinating from his submarine headquarters would both help Warrior Life and hurt Warrior Reformer in the same punch. What was left of WR, as the bitch-ass faction was known, after their top ranks were killed off internally, would be quickly hunted down and killed off by the proper authorities, based in large part on Warrior Life's tips. It was his own countersurveillance that had first hatched the plot when they discovered WR was looking at one bank with multinational political connections in the accounts they held—another move from G-Money's playbook. With an idiot plan in place, he would let them walk in and rob this bank. He'd even help them by disabling the four cellular alarms that went out to the usual 211 cop code lines, leaving these idiots to spend hours locked away in a vault that held no money of any value, other than the bait million, while Warrior Life's expert crews hit seven of LA's most valuable Mob-run banks in the process.

As for taking pages from other players' books, G-Money had stolen this one straight out of the Joker's, when he'd decided to use the opportunity to reorganize the laundering of seven of the world's biggest Mafia-owned banks' operations. Each was controlled by one of the biggest crime families in the country and the world. The three that had infiltrated the United States successfully for long enough to still be standing were the Russians and Mexicans, as the Italians controlled the other five. In total, the world's leading crime syndicates that weren't under Warrior Life's control would seize controlling interest in the five New York crime families, including such veterans as the Gambino, Genovese, Bonanno, Colombo, and Lucchese families, as well as the Mogilevich Russian Mafia, the Guzman crime family headed by jailed boss El Chapo, and the Pacific Rim's leader, who represented the Japanese, Chinese, and other Asian Mob factions in the US money-laundering world, the Wing-hung family.

Rather than stealing their money, he was protecting it, and in the biggest transfer of wealth in modern organized crime, G-Money transferred half of the remaining balance in to Warrior Life cryptocurrency, while moving the other 45 percent to Switzerland, where they could collect and reorganize outside the US banking system. G-Money would gain allies from the move on the legal side of the shareholder banking circuit around the globe, even as the United States felt a near-earthquake of panic among their greedy shareholders. For decades, these leeches had knowingly taken profits off commissions from laundering these criminal networks' money, and they took those profits and paid political donations to the politicians and law enforcement networks that fought to stop the flow of this river of commerce.

Money was like water, a fitting context for the backdrop in which G-Money operated, and as he took personal phone calls from the heads of these furious seven families, explaining, in his dominant Jamaican accent, how close they'd come to losing hundreds of millions, moods calmed as the bosses realized the majority of their money was safe—not only safe but more valuable as part of the Warrior Life crypto network. These were men steeled in the price of doing business and too well trained through watching their best friends and loved ones die for them to take it personally. As G-Money gave them their latest lesson, he internally was surprised at how easily they took the spanking. They knew it as a cost of business, and every once in a while, to stay on top, they knew they had to pay. G-Money advertised himself as a partner, not a superior, and this made the pain much easier to absorb, as seven banks were robbed of money that the government could have seized at any time anyway.

Back on the streets, the bumper stickers read as clearly as they needed to: *Warrior Reformer*, with red spray paint through the word *Reformer*, *Life* custom-painted in white over the top, and *rat* tattooed across the forehead of G-Currency's face on the right of each bumper sticker, just across from Christopher Columbus's on the left. T-shirts were given away at every swap-meet, club, community meeting, and church service, and soon, G-Currency was in the hands of Warrior Life soldiers, on his way to an execution in the heart of his own turf.

One of G-Money's most trusted West Coast generals was OG Compton, who had helped G-Money organize the street gangs a decade earlier. Here, he would cement his position as G-Money's top dog on the West Coast, and he'd proved himself a talent in picking colorful ways to announce his authority after he'd requested—and received—permission to debut one of Warrior Life's latest dazzling innovations in weaponry. The common military soldiery, from the infantry on up through the Special Forces, didn't even know they had it at their disposal when the M4 CQBR hit the hands of his Warrior Life soldiers.

One of the fringes, the WL crew, got every new hot car on the market to test drive in excursions; most military operators dreamed of being a part of such tests but rarely got the green light to put their training into action. Along with being paid and protected better than the world's best mercenaries, they were given the latest hardware that the manufacturers had to brag about long before they reached military weapons contractors or, more locally, gun shows. It ranged from the M4A1 to the M16A4 to the HK416 to the MK16 Mod, MK 17, right down to the M27 infantry automatic rifle. G-Money test-fired every one of those bitches himself, shredding everything from great white sharks to even a few select traitors he had personally brought to his legendry planks.

Like every pirate, G-Money had planks, though rather than ships, his extended off his sub out into the open sea, usually with plenty of well-baited sharks and related man-eating fish fear-swimming around below, giving his traitors and enemies plenty to think about as he marched them off into the abyss. G-Money always thought of Jabba and the Tatooine desert monster Sarlacc, eating his prey as they confessed before a certain fate. There would be no R2-D2 with a light saber here. Warrior Life's traitors were fed to the fish on a weekly basis, usually on a candid camera, when G-Money's face and sub weren't in view. Today, however, he made a special exception, appearing before the hologram exterior of his very own pirate ship. Of course, it was an illusion to viewers but real enough to resonate with his viewers that the plank was his own, and the cattle prods that pushed his bitches out toward their fate as they begged G-Money for their lives were as real as any man's mortality ever gets.

G-Currency was no different—he trembled and cried like a woman as he sat in the heart of the Bermuda Triangle, the real G-spot, getting ready to be swallowed up by Pussy, off the coast of the United States—and on the East Coast, no less, which probably offended his West Coast sensibilities even further. G-Money always sought to drive the knife into traitors as deeply as possible, hitting them in the nerve center of the foolish impulse they'd had to betray him or test him. It was a relief that G-Currency wasn't a member of his inner circle that he was having to execute; rather, he was an external rival, the kind of rebel he welcomed the opportunity to crush like a fucking flaming meteor.

The world soon would be watching what was being filmed now by trusty drones, which were the Spielbergs of electronic film, with Daco directing. G-Money relished these rare opportunities for direct confrontation. G-Money, wearing his customary skeleton-painted ski mask with *WL* printed across the front, sentenced G-Currency to death before the watching world, with black markets taking live bets as the sentence unfolded.

"Currency, why you put a G before your name?" G-Money demanded. "That's the same as putting yourself before *God*, and you will be judged today accordingly. Never betray Warrior Life. It's the next chapter in the Bible, and you are about to be next! Being merciful, I give you a choice of feeling one blade—or hundreds waiting you below with the sharks."

"I worship you, G-Money! Spare my life!" G-Currency pleaded.

"I don't need to hear you beg, bruh. You're weaker than a whimper before me, before Warrior Life worldwide! You bitches die so we can live. I hereby sentence you to death, first by beheading, and then what's left of you will be eaten alive by the nature of God."

Slicing downward with the mastery of a samurai, with one decisive slice, G-Money cleanly separated Currency's head from the rest of his bitch ass. The sharks happily feasted, which logged one hundred million views by the end of the weekend. Of course, the final frame of the viral video read, WARRIOR LIFE RULES!

CHAPTER 6

PRANKING MCNAIR

G-Money's favorite hobby was pranking McNair—hands down. He'd first done it a decade earlier, when they had him strapped down in the psych ward, and he'd been sending him on wild goose chases ever since. His favorite kind came with sightings of the world's most wanted fugitive in major metropolitan cities, requiring enormous expenditures in human, technical, and equipment resources that ultimately cost McNair, both in embarrassing front-page headlines and huge reimbursement bills, once the invoices from the cities' fire departments, police departments, SWAT, and fugitive squads, reached his desk.

Under the guise of national security, McNair operated with a huge budget, by any other fugitive hunter's standards, but with so many resources devoted to hunting the head of one network, G-Money's bill to the US government so far had exceeded the hunt for bin Laden's by double. He would keep tapping those bitches for billions over the next ten years. As Warrior Life's networks became more sophisticated with technology's own advancements, it cost law enforcement that much more to keep up with the hunt, even though, privately, any head of the multiple agencies hunting G-Money and his network on different fronts would admit they were at least two years behind whatever technology Warrior Life was using, and they always cooked their books internally to underwrite at least 25 percent of the cost of the hunt, or they'd all have been fired years earlier.

The fact that McNair still held his position was simply a matter of his having a job nobody else wanted. G-Money had punked McNair in public so many times that it had become a vendetta at this point. Even though the top spy agencies around the globe wanted G-Money because of what he had in his head, McNair had sworn—off the record—to kill him on sight, if given the shot. McNair had a wanted poster with a special bull's-eye, which he'd personally paid a poster printing service to create for him. He hung it on the back of his office door, which was most times closed. The target had G-Money's face in the middle, a classic wanted poster–style framed the rest of his target. At the beginning of every day, he nursed another hangover with his favorite morning cocktail—$1000 single malt scotch from the case G-Money sent to him every year on the anniversary of his escape from the psych ward. He mixed it with a cup of kopi luwak, which currently was the world's most expensive coffee from Vietnam, selling for between $100 and $500 per pound, another fringe benefit of the hunt for G-Money, which routinely arrived once a month by drone-drop with a handwritten note: "To keep you fresh for the day's hunt! Peace. G-Money."

McNair hated to admit it, but like the FBI supervising agent in *The Sopranos* who received a yearly gift from Tony Soprano's Satriale's Pork Store, he had many fringe benefits from the hunt for Warrior Life and pranks that made him laugh as hard as G-Money did when he opened a new box of cigars from Cuba or a case of sake for McNair's team. Sometimes, he even sneaked in box seats at a Super Bowl or World Series.

G-Money sent these taunting gestures of kindness randomly, and often, as a "fuck you" of sorts to McNair to show how his network continued to thrive, even as it was the world's most hunted, as well as a sign of the begrudging respect both men had developed for one another over the past ten years. G-Money was the Joe Carroll to McNair's Ryan Hardy; the Neil McCauley to Vincent Hanna (in *Heat*); the Ted Bundy to Robert D. Keppel (the detective who eventually caught the serial killer. Still, no matter how determined McNair was, he'd never catch G-Money, and privately, he'd started to believe that too. It was the worst doubt a manhunter could ever feel, equivalent to a boxer who has lost his confidence in the ring on the night of a title fight. McNair nonetheless rose every morning to face the fight another day. It was the only fight he had left in him, one that would be career-defining, whether he caught G-Money or not. For anyone else in McNair's position, it would be the worst kind of assignment given to a veteran federal law enforcement agent, the equivalent of manning an air tower in Alaska.

Still, the sublevel, Siberianesque basement from which McNair ran his worldwide manhunt for G-Money had some charm. He was left alone by his superiors most the time, and while his superiors, in public, often castigated him, he'd survived two FBI directors and two presidents in the past ten years. Truthfully, McNair knew too much to be fired, and he was the only law enforcement veteran of his experience who would take the gig—again, because he couldn't get another if he'd paid a million dollars for the assignment. Raising his favorite coffee mug to his lot in life as he sat across the room from the bull's-eye poster, McNair downed the coffee-scotch blend in one long gulp before begrudgingly opening his latest email with supposed intel on a Warrior Life cell operating in Cleveland.

McNair had a plane on stand-by, and from his basement lair, he felt a little like Batman in the Batcave, as if the sighting hotline sounded, he could deploy within two minutes by speedboat—specifically his own fleet of WP-18 tactical strike craft. The world's fastest known naval boat, the Special Forces Interceptor speedboats traveled at hundreds of miles per hour and were outfitted with retractable remote weapons, mounted with a 30mm cannons, small SAM or SSM launchers in the bow, two retractable Rheinmetall ROSY (Rapid Obscuring System) soft-kill systems, and a retractable EO mast. They could rocket toward justice from the underwater canals the Bureau had constructed back in the 1960s, which dumped into the Potomac and, soon thereafter, the Atlantic Ocean, if McNair's fleet of state-of-the-art speedboats needed to intercept a smuggling tip at sea.

They could respond by air, if they needed to, courtesy of the latest and greatest in high-speed military choppers on stand-by. Within three minutes from headquarters, McNair could board one of his beloved Ka-52 "Alligator" choppers, which flew at maximum speeds of 300 kilometers per hour, making it one of the fastest in the world. And of course, the one that gave him a hard-on every time he looked at it, the Mi-28N Night Hunter—he had three, which were originally designed for search-and-destroy operations, whether facing armored vehicles, tanks, or even missiles. Able to fly day or night in any weather, it could hold its own in a speed contest with the Ka-52 and the NH90.

McNair's chief equipment man was nicknamed "Bodies" by the crew because of his official body count, hanging among the military jerseys in the rafters of their proverbial arena of greatest warriors.

Bodies was alternately known by his service jacket as Gianni Giuseppe Bodatelli, and even though he was African American, his father was unknown and his mother was a white Italian woman, banished from an organized crime family, once she'd been knocked up by a black hustler. Bodies, aka OG Mac Dog, had been raised in the streets of Brooklyn by a den of pimps, and he and G-Money had been running together since they were in grade school, learning all the hustling trades on the front lines of the warzone that Bed-Stuy was back then.

OG Mac Dog was G-Money's personal plant inside McNair's twelve-person manhunter team, all experts from various branches of the military. They also all had pasts that involved lots of professional extractions and assassinations for Uncle Sam, from rescues of US soldiers captured behind enemy lines, to the extractions of prisoners the US government wanted and who had to be broken out of foreign prisons, and every kind of operation in between. McNair had chosen each of the twelve personally, including OG Mac Dog, known by his cover identity as a former Navy SEAL captain who, at age thirty, was one of the most lethal killers among the group. He'd racked up forty-nine kills in his twelve years in the service. Unbeknownst to McNair, he had logged his first twenty in the first two years he'd been part of a covert Iraq border terrorist-hunting squad, alongside G-Money, his partner and lifelong best friend. OG Mac Dog was one of his most loyal soldiers.

Because both had come up in the foster system, their records had been sealed and then erased entirely by G-Money's hackers after he'd gone on the run. While OG Mac Dog's record of military service was 100 percent legitimate for the past decade, his first two years were buried deep in the military's most classified files. McNair had brought him in personally at the recommendation of a highly respected Europe section chief from the CIA, who'd run Middle Eastern operations for the agency during the first five years of the war on terrorism in the early 2000s. G-Money and OG Mac Dog had been two of his most lethal operators along the border, and when G-Money supposedly was killed in action—according to his military record, anyway—along with the rest of their unit, Mac Dog had been the only member of the elite unit to walk out of the smoke and sandstorm alive.

Just as G-Money had gone underground, Mac Dog was given his choice of service anywhere in the world with any branch. Ready for a return to the States, his and McNair's paths had crossed at the perfect point in the destiny of both men. McNair needed a professional of Mac Dog's lethal reach, up close and far away, where weaponry was concerned. Like an untrained mechanic who could start any car when he got under the hood, Mac Dog's natural acumen for military equipment had outfitted McNair's entire arsenal over the past decade. He never made a purchase without first consulting Bodies's opinion, no matter how cool it sounded, looked, or fired, and Mac Dog was now his second in command because he simply relied on that expertise.

Bodies's position in the hierarchy of McNair's private army gave him the position to keep McNair just current enough to be a necessary step behind G-Money and Warrior Life, whenever new equipment was acquired. If McNair's unit got a new piece of satellite spying gear, OG Daco was immediately notified so he could acquire whatever was necessary to combat it. Today's wild goose chase would be courtesy of a well-planted tip from Interpol, one that would sound like instant gold to a less-experienced victim of G-Money's false leads, so he had to make this one look especially good.

He and Daco had sat in their control center on the sub, smoking a Bob Marley–sized joint of the latest strain from their private garden of the world's finest marijuana, as they planned it out.

The city they'd picked to fuck with this month was Providence, Rhode Island, the latest to be outfitted with a Homeland Security upgrade to its infrastructure against hacking, and Daco was dying to put his own counter-defenses to the test. He hadn't had to beg G-Money to spend Warrior Life resources on the project, once he explained its proximity along the Eastern Seaboard to Washington, DC, where McNair was stationed and would be deployed, once the Warrior Life electronic hacking signature was identified by US intelligence services. All the usual alarm bells would sound, but even better, because this city was ahead of its first official training with their new equipment, it would cost a couple of extra million to the city and, ultimately, to McNair's budget. Headlines would bring Warrior Life soldiers crawling out of the woodwork in the process, once word got out that G-Money's network had pulled off the latest hack of the city's grids.

Daco's plan was brilliant in its simplicity—phone in, through an untraceable ghost network of cellular lines, a nuclear bomb threat to city hall, which happened to be located within the same two-block radius as the city's court buildings, police headquarters, and city jail. Because it doubled as an unofficial federal holding facility on the top floor for high-profile US government witnesses for various criminal trials around the country, G-Money would be extracting several prisoners from pending testimony that day, as Bodies personally executed each of them, while McNair and other team members raided floors below in search of Warrior Life's on-the-ground soljas. G-Money always had at least one Warrior Life solja on the site of each prank call to coordinate ground operations—or chaos within—of the appropriate Warrior Life spray painting on the walls of the bosses' offices, wanted posters of G-Money and associates, and anywhere else that would be officially embarrassing.

They would catch the city with its pants down, they would really be spanked once the live feed of the chaos was mysteriously uploaded onto the news sites of every major local and national cable news network. The concert of mayhem that Daco conducted—an excited symphony of typing on his eight keyboards across a cyber concert of confusion—played that much prettier as G-Money watched it unfold in real time. Police cars crashed into civilians as Daco turned the traffic lights at major downtown intersections from green to red and red to green, seemingly without reason, with the push of a few buttons.

G-Money spotted the fine booty of one of his bodyguards leaning over a monitor to watch closer. Before long, he was rocking her as they laughed their asses off together at the controlled chaos that was overtaking the peaceful seaside city.

Soon, smoke billowed from the cell windows over multiple floors of the city's towering jail complex, as military helicopters landed on helipads on its roof. Hovering news choppers captured McNair and his Warrior Life manhunting force hopping out in full assault mode. When he discovered the doors to the complex had been welded shut, McNair and company rappelled down the sides of the structure to the eighth floor, where explosives knocked out a section of reinforced windows as they made entry.

In a way, G-Money was making McNair look like Rambo on the live news in the middle of the day, as he needed his most committed pursuer to stay in power. Shows of force like this kept him popular enough with the public to keep any politician from daring to unseat him.

Nodding to Daco, G-Money green-lit the execution/extraction portion of the operation, as Bodies, aka OG Mac Dog, received a preprogrammed signal in the beacon embedded in his neck to activate the Warrior Life operation. While chaos enveloped the building below, on the top floor, Mac Dog—with Daco hacking into the federal level of the jail's cell blocks to automatically open all cell doors—walked from cell to cell, executing those traitors who were scheduled to testify against Warrior Life affiliates, along with five extra targets that Mob bosses around the country had paid G-Money's network an extra $100 million in cash to silence from their pending testimony.

Of the fifteen prisoners on the block, five were left safely in their bullet-proof cells, with doors locked, for Bodies to safely rescue. At the same time, the two guards on duty were executed and their automatic rifles placed in the hands of two of the dead prisoners. Daco cut the security feed long enough for Mac Dog to reposition the bodies in the hall so it looked like an assault on the guards had caught the eight other dead bodies in the crossfire, a result of their storming the hallway when their cell doors opened.

After the smoke cleared and the dust settled, no bombs would be found, except one in the office of the facility's warden, automatically disabled once the bomb squad sent in their robot, with a Joker's laugh straight out of *Batman* to let those bitches know they'd been had. With a hologram of G-Money that was reminiscent of Princess Leia's beaming out of R2-D2 at the start of *Star Wars*, G-Money delivered his latest decree, declaration, and demands to US law enforcement, as well as the usual taunt to McNair personally and a total for the citizens of providence for the damages they would be charged by the city as taxpayers. Today's bill was $37 million, and as McNair broke his hand for the fourth time in ten years, slamming it into a steel wall as he watched G-Money's latest untraceable holographic message, he swore he'd kill the little bastard with his own hands when this one heeled. He had so much adrenaline surging through him that he swore he could do it even with his broken hand.

He felt the phone ring in his left hip pocket, and that only occurred when his superiors were watching another embarrassment to the federal authorities unfold, live, on television. A shouting match ensued, in which McNair placed the blame on the locals, on whose technical infrastructure his people had relied for their own intel. Because it had been hacked by Warrior Life, no one was truly to blame, but McNair knew his boss was yelling at him on a conference call with several other superiors because they needed to watch somebody's ass get chewed out live, in the moment. Most of them wouldn't have had the balls to even speak to McNair that way in person, for fear he'd have ripped their throats out, just as he fantasized doing to G-Money. Over many years and embarrassments of this sort, he'd learned not to take it personally.

As professionally as possible, he yes-sir'd his superiors, even as they saw his hand bleeding and suggested he should get it serviced by medical personnel. McNair ignored the pain long enough to swear a new level of resolve to catch G-Money, just what his superiors needed to see from the man they knew they could not replace. It was an act for the cameras at that point in the ten-year manhunt that they privately would admit—to a wife or priest or mistress—was beginning to wear them all down. At the same time, they knew it was the one thing they could never admit publicly— that G-Money had beaten them: outmanned, outgunned, outhacked, outmaneuvered at every turn. It was the perfect racket because none could afford to report it.

As McNair watched the sun set over the beautiful coast that he'd raced up that morning, he headed home to his divorced, empty existence in an apartment appropriately rented in the Watergate, while his wife and three children ate dinner with their new stepfather in his real home, not three miles away. McNair steamed at the shit pile his life had become over the past decade. G-Money had cost him everything: his professional reputation, his personal life after he'd lost his family, and his sobriety after he'd broken his twenty-year-record of not drinking when G-Money had escaped the psych ward in what still counted above Ruby Ridge or Waco as the FBI's most embarrassing public humiliation in the Bureau's history.

Today, McNair would add another sad chapter to that official record. Still, he knew that none of his superiors had the balls or authority to fire him. That order could only come from the president of the United States, and although McNair was unaware, G-Money was about to make an unwitting ally of her, thanks to a private embarrassment with as major a public disgrace as the one McNair and the FBI had just suffered.

CHAPTER 7

PRESIDENT LESBIAN

MANY OF G-MONEY'S MOST LOYAL government plants, throughout his worldwide network of informants, had come at the very top levels of elected government—senators who controlled purse strings for the budgets appropriated through Congress to hunt Warrior Life around the globe. He could simply buy off most of them by making them partners, but some were so self-righteous that he had to catch them in their acts of immorality before they would realize they had no other choice but to bow down to G-Money to ensure their own survival.

Tonight, he was about to snare his biggest catch to date, a sitting US president, a notorious poon hound who made Bill Clinton and Donald Trump look like choir boys. Boy, would he have this dick singing where he'd been swinging just a few hours earlier. Presidents naively thought they were above reproach when they got elected because following Trump's porn stars and pussy-grabbing, the country had taken a decidedly moral turn in the road in the next election, electing an African American Mormon to office, the first of that political pedigree and one whose wife was even more popular than the president—more popular than Jackie O. or even Eleanor Roosevelt.

Tonight, he'd catch her in bed with her wife and a third woman. Yes, the new president was a woman, and she and her wife were wild about three-ways in the Lincoln bedroom.

G-Money's plant in the Secret Service had already wired the room with Daco's personally designed gnat-drone cameras—fascinating, in that they could sit silently on the wall, smaller than the size of a fly, and still capture a movie-theater–sized screen of embarrassment for the unfortunate star of the scene. Tonight, there were ten such bugs placed for sound and screen throughout the room as G-Money fucked two of his finest hoes and watched the orgy unfold in the Oval Office. He'd come up with the headline the night before, "Orgy in the Oval Office," that he'd present the president and her First Lady with when running down their options later on that night. For now, he let them have their fun.

He'd personally overseen the training of his own Warrior Life Secret Service plant, watched her lick one hundred pussies until she got his technique just right, tight, the best in the world by professional porn graders, as she needed to pull off the coup of the twenty-first century to land the role she was playing tonight. G-Money watched as two of his finest hoes licked each other's pussies for a captive audience around the sub, the personnel not on duty, while on a candid camera, he captured the president of the United States—a mere year into office—in a scandalous orgy. While everyone charged with prosecuting and impeaching her privately would find it hot, they'd all publicly decry it at the loudest levels. The religious reverberations alone would kill her base of voter support after the Mormon Church excommunicated her.

Then there would be the voter fallout within her home state of Utah, and it would spread faster than AIDS had in Africa, before G-Money had cured the continent of the plague.

He'd smiled that morning, seeing the stock rise in the new miracle, which was privately funded and owned by Warrior Life, as it hit the market. It would save generations of lives around Africa, and G-Money had agreed to make the vaccine free to every country on the continent in exchange for private pledges of passage, legally and illegally, where his myriad business interests were concerned, and publicly, where each vial of vaccine, supplied by G-Money's Warrior Life labs or not at all, was officially stamped with the WL logo. This had infuriated industrialized governments around the globe, especially when Warrior Life had contacted each with Don Corleone–style impossible-to-refuse license deals to distribute the vaccine in their respective countries. With the threat of alerting the media to the fact these governments had quarreled over any price demanded against their own capitalistic pharmaceutical backdrops for a cure to the world's most deadly diseases, they'd ultimately agreed to pay whatever price—on the front and back ends—that G-Money had demanded for initial supplies, as well as resupplying the vaccine.

Snapping from his stock screen back to his live Washington porn feed as he watched the POTUS skillfully work her First Lady's pussy with one hand while she twisted the Secret Service woman's nipples hard with the other, with a thirteen-inch black dildo fucking her ample ass in the interim, G-Money had to admit that in another life, this president could have been a porn star.

"Wait!" He laughed out loud. "She *is* a porn star!" As of that minute, Warrior Life owned the White House, and there was plenty of room for more African American female advancement within the US government in the years to come, as G-Money would help to secure her second term under his own terms of office. He was running shit like Pac would have, to the fullest, and as he spent the next couple of hours running a train on seven of his finest Warrior Life fems, he planted the seed of his next unborn son, just as he watched all three ladies cum to multiple orgasms in what would soon be, for the four of them, their own little secret.

Tapping the asses of each of his ladies dry, G-Money signaled for the next shift of tech folks to take their places at their command posts, as he and Daco—who'd banged hundreds of women within G-Money's presence, and vice versa—tallied up their respective scorecards on the latest round of pounds, rich betting among Warrior Life scoreboards on G-Money's latest conquests. Of course, he got a piece of all the action and decided that the fact they had done it in real time with the president of the United States' own orgy would be worth an extra point across the spread. Turning to business, as he took another deep drag of the latest strain of killer bud fogging up their submarine, G-Money prepared to hit up the president in her post-orgy glory with a little video recap that would buy her lifelong loyalty.

Just as she stepped into the shower, the president's private nuclear-security video phone rang. She grabbed a robe, ran her hands through her hair, and hit the "accept call" screen, expecting to find the Joint Chief of Staff general or chief of staff with some midnight crisis that came with the job. Instead, she saw a face that she'd seen only on wanted posters while touring the FBI. Today, she'd meet her greatest nemesis and ally, both in one in person, via video from halfway around the globe. She seemed speechless when he greeted her, not with his own face but with a quickly edited highlight reel of her past three hours of pleasure, and pain seemed to shoot through her like a lightning bolt. She sat on the shower's tiled bench as G-Money suddenly popped up in front of her widening eyes. In a thick Jamaican accent, he greeted her in a man-to-man way, which, as she'd write in her memoirs, ultimately made her a stronger leader after the moment of truth had arrived, dealing with the male-dominated military hierarchy going forward.

"What's happenin', sexy Ma?" G-Money said. "G-Money reaching out personally to let you know how much I enjoyed watching your three-way freeway of pleasure, Ma. Never seen a woman, let alone a politician, take a thirteen-inch dildo in the ass so easily, Ma! I bet the whole world would *love* to watch that, say, a billion times over in the first twenty-four hours, Ma. I bet it would make the Guinness World Records. Shall I go on, Ma? You want the rest of the world to see this or keep it our little secret?"

The president, red-faced and silent, closed her eyes for the longest thirty seconds of her life as she watched her past political life—everything she'd endured; every smelly, redneck hand she'd shaken up to this point in her life—evaporate in ten brutal seconds, with two for breathing and another ten for how, historically, she'd be the next Richard Nixon. She took the final eight seconds to compose herself.

Finally, President Haywood responded, showing her famous sexy smile that G-Money had seen in a million campaign ads. "Mr. G-Money, we finally meet. I've gotten to know you over my last year of daily briefings. And to think I almost didn't believe you were real."

"I'm not Shakespeare, dear. I'm as real as that video, and the rest of the world can feel me, if you don't. I have a simple proposition; it's one that many of your colleagues around the world, sitting right where you are now, have been given as they got to know me over their first few years of power. I can keep you there, like I did them, or I can take you down with this tape before your first term is even started. You know it, and I know it; the only point is what we both want—for me to stay on the run. The longer I'm on the run, the longer you stay in power. That simple."

President Haywood cleared her throat. She saw in her mind—with all the power of projection that had delivered her this far—that she had no choice. She was prepared to negotiate. "I only have so much power, as I'm sure you appreciate. The government runs much deeper than my control, from the UFO program to the CIA, where they've previously removed presidents from power, if you remember Kennedy."

"You have one job: keep McNair in charge—that's it. You can throw as much money and hatred at me as you want, Ma; in fact, I expect you to call a press conference in the morning from the Oval Office to declare Warrior Life officially on the US International Terrorism Watchlist. We're already on the US, but now, we'll be hunted, officially, by a coordinated effort you'll be heading. I'll promise lots of snacks in the next few years—major narco traffickers your administration can take credit for capturing, killing, and dismantling. The price is simple: G-Money stays free. I have everything I need to fight my fight. You need to make me your fight. Make G-Money Public Enemy No. 1. The more it looks like you're hunting me, the more any suspicion will point away."

"And the video?" President Haywood asked. "If my daughter saw that, let alone my church or the country …"

"Rest easy, Ma," G-Money told her. "It will never make its way into the National Archives—unless I'm caught!" He laughed.

"I can't control McNair," President Haywood objected.

"I don't want him controlled! He's a junkyard dog I want off the leash. The wilder and crazier he gets, the better you look—trust me. I'll take care of McNair; you take care of the press. Warrior Life should be bigger than Al Capone to you—the new war on crime! Trust me, Prez; it will secure your second term and give you the one thing you've always missed with voters: a tough record on crime. I'll take care of the rest, but if I ever step foot on US soil—anywhere around the world, in any interrogation room—you will get that call, and you'll know what to say: that G-Money can never set foot on US soil again. This way, your little secret will stay safely between the two of us. BTW, Prez—*love* how you take the thirteen-inch kielbasa!"

The president watched the screen go blank, and as the steam cleared from her shower, her mind was as clear as a cloudless summer day: this video could never see the light of day. She now had her own personal political scandal to contain. Her odds were better than Nixon's—she knew that—but she couldn't risk becoming the next Bill Clinton. Even if she survived it politically, she never would personally, and the First Lady was too important to her to ever lose her. G-Money had assured her she could keep her present Secret Service company too, for both their security. Suddenly, she felt a strange weight lift. She went to bed and drifted off to sleep. She had a big day in the morning, declaring a new war on crime against Warrior Life. G-Money would become the most famous wanted man on earth, more infamous than Al Capone or Charlie Manson. G-Money was now a living god. *God Money.*

CHAPTER 8

WARRIOR LIFE DUPPY SQUAD

THE AIR OFF THE COAST of Jamaica looked and smelled like a mist of marijuana. It was almost green at night when a lighthouse beam shone across it.

The headlights of G-Money's Warrior Life Duppy Squad were presently off. They sat low in their speedboats, talking with one of G-Money's top lieutenants about a submarine, as the finest Rasta grass the island had grown was loaded in front of their eyes. One of Daco's remotely controlled subs in G-Money's fleet of manned and unmanned underwater crafts would be the envy of any country's navy. He transported hundreds of pounds throughout the Caribbean to destinations abroad that could be reached only by such an elite fleet.

G-Money's drone subs each came equipped with self-destruct functions, controllable from his mother ship. In over ten years, G-Money had only had to deploy two from the hundreds of runs around the globe, as the lead trafficker of the finest imported marijuana seeds, strains, oils, and hundreds of thousands of pounds of the good old-fashioned "wacky tabacky."

Whenever he was intercepted, he would dispatch one of his drone subs to sink the entire fleet of whatever coast guard had cost him money. Whether the customer or law enforcement covered the loss, somebody always paid. Tonight, Warrior Life was transporting the last of the season's harvest, just before the island shut down for the winter months.

Contrary to popular tourist belief, Jamaica had winter months, at least where traditional farming harvests were concerned, even if the tourists populated their beaches year-round. G-Money had a private island of his own off the northwestern coast of Jamaica, facing a perfect escape port between Santiago and Haiti, if needed, but G-Money had never had to flee. He was protected by the Duppy Squad, Jamaica's most feared ghost army in local lore, passed down from generation to generation throughout the island culture.

G-Money had first struck the pact with Marlon "Duppy Film" Perry, once dubbed Jamaica's most wanted man, ten years earlier, when he'd been in charge of the underground Duppy Squad that G-Money now commanded. He'd personally beheaded Perry after staging what looked like—to the public—a police raid, during which he'd been executed. In fact, the manhunt had been a ruse for Warrior Life's soldiers to abduct Perry and bring him back to kneel before G-Money and beg for his traitor life.

G-Money, on film, got Perry to admit he'd tried to rat the world's most wanted man to the Jamaican army's intelligence services, who, in turn, had tipped Warrior Life and led to Perry's capture and demise. The video had gone viral on the black web, and the Duppy Squad was soon absorbed, like a subsidiary of G-Money's armed forces.

The history of the Duppy Squad was a fascinating one to G-Money that he had no intention of rewriting, neither in its charter nor in its ways of doing things to keep the locals in line. If anything, G-Money delegated down the chain so as not to interrupt any of the cultural pillars Duppy held higher than any other transcendental traditions or superstitions.

Originally rooted in Bantu folklore, Bob Marley had even written a theme, "Duppy Conqueror," while other popular reggae artists from the island had scored musical tributes, from Bunny Wailer's "Duppy Gun," to Ernie Smith's "Duppy Gunman," Yellowman's album *Duppy Or Gunman,* Chase & Status's "Duppy Men," and dancehall star Demarco's hit single, "Duppy Know Who Fi Frighten." A ghost army was precisely what G-Money had been drawn to when he'd initially infiltrated and then took over Jamaica's marijuana growing and trafficking operations.

Perry's beheading had brought everyone in line, and he'd spent the past few years making them richer and more protected from law enforcement than ever before. The crime rate had dropped around the island, and tourism had provided a ready customer source for samples of new product. Often, G-Money would set prices for different strains, based on how well they performed with the white tourist crowd from around the globe. He'd also doubled the Duppy's annual take from the marijuana trade—a benefit from streamlining island operations under one new order that they maintained on the ground. Nobody stole from the Duppy, and the Duppy, in turn, wouldn't dare steal from G-Money. Even law enforcement's budgets had increased due to the healthy river of bribes flowing through the island's easygoing culture.

The real challenge had been the coast guard, who coordinated their patrols with international counterparts from the drug interdiction and maritime law enforcement apparatus, run largely by incorruptible, righteous do-gooders who actually took their oath to uphold the law seriously. G-Money knew better than to laugh off these people. They were professionals and probably were his only serious competition on the open seas anymore. Getting through the port exits and onto the open Caribbean had become more and more challenging on the water's surface over the years, whether a speedboat or oil tanker, so G-Money's revolutionary fleet of drone subs, with 100 percent sonar satellite masking, had been the best investment he'd made in his vast military equipment budget over the past decade.

Boots on the ground and drones in the water and overhead had long been G-Money's philosophy for keeping the scales balanced, and he'd taken his Warrior Life Duppy hit squads global after first taking over their operations in Jamaica. Duppy was a code word, of sorts, for an elite force of assassins who could strike anywhere, anytime—almost like ghosts, as they struck in silence. Often, theirs were last faces their victims saw before death and the last they'd ever expect to see—the farthest thing from the stereotypical movie hitmen.

G-Money often recruited with a suicide-bomber mentality, although he drew the line at killing innocent bystanders. His targets were always person-specific and carried out by those who society had cast to live in its shadows anyway. In the United States, they often posed as homeless vets who were, in fact, homeless vets, those who G-Money first had tried to save through mental and medical treatments. For those who had terminal physical or mental injuries, joining Warrior Life's Duppy Squad meant dying with a certain honor that society had stripped from them when they'd returned home and wound up living on the streets.

As a fellow veteran, G-Money had driven homelessness among veterans down to a ten-year low, as he recruited many into Warrior Life and took them off the streets. Those who left and came back did so by choice, after months of rest and rehabilitation at one of G-Money's private island resorts in the Caribbean. They wore the rags they attacked in like a uniform, and they saw the streets as a battlefield on which they were to make their last stand. The targets were always high profile, fitting the psychological resurrection of honor for which a fallen soldier needed to stand and fight. In the process, they rid the world of many of its ugliest characters, where governments couldn't, such as a sex trafficker whose throat was slit in the alley of a hotel in a country where he thought he was above the law and probably untouchable—except by a highly trained ghost hitter from the Warrior Life Duppy Squad.

These kamikaze heroes always went out on their kill missions voluntarily and from the shadows, where they were ignored anyway. They wore the most brilliant disguise that assassins arguably could ever hide out in, and there were never witnesses among the real homeless because these killers had been recruited from among their own. Warrior Life was generous with the donations too—money, the finest alcohol, drugs—that they could never afford. For those Duppy Squad soldiers who knew their next mission was their last, a sense of pride came with avenging their fellow homeless brethren.

Tonight's hit was a corrupt general, Selvandieu Abbé, of the Haitian army, who had enslaved homeless refugee women following the hurricanes that devastated the island, while leaving their husbands, children, and loved ones to die in the street. G-Money had recruited, from among their husbands, one hundred volunteers for this evening's mission. Many of them knew they might not make it out, but the thought of freeing their wives, sisters, mothers, and others taken hostage by the general was worth whatever risk they faced to their own lives. Warrior Life had promised to take care of their families, and G-Money had deposited a million in Warrior Life cryptocurrency, per man, to ensure their peace of mind, as a still mind was required to carry out such stealth. They moved from the shadows into the light just long enough to snatch the life from the selected target, like a zombie, or a vampire, or whatever other nightmare forms the Duppy Squad took on to their victims. Tonight, a new chapter of legends would be born.

Because the Haitians believed in the existence of zombies, voodoo (even though it was officially outlawed in 1934 with the Christian missionary invasion), and other black magic beliefs among the local island culture, it made for a perfect segue for the Duppy to become a living part of that culture. After they struck tonight, freeing hundreds of sexually enslaved women, they would become a permanent and welcome addition to Haiti's mysterious spiritual system. The strike point was the general's compound at Fort Rivière, originally built by the French in the 1800s and, ironically, once the site of a famed battle between rebels and US Marines in 1915. Tonight, 103 years later, it was occupied by General Abbé, who had seized it in a coup when the government was in upheaval, following Hurricane Matthew two years earlier.

After hearing rumors of screams that echoed off the ocean for miles and living quarters that had been turned into rape dens, the newly recruited local Duppy assassins could already taste the general's blood in their mouths, just as they could taste their wives' kisses. Some of these soldiers had dreams of reunions and life on the beach in paradise after freeing their loved ones from their current captivity.

Still others knew this was a kamikaze mission in every sense of the word, and most of the men fighting on the battlefield tonight knew they would die with honor, freeing their loved ones, who would forgive them afterward because they died for their loved ones' freedom. While they walked through the valleys of the shadows and into position, the lazy guards in towers above picked up nothing on radar, thanks to Warrior Life's latest toy: stealth suits. They were designed by a fugitive whom Warrior Life had picked up during a routine prisoner transfer, which had turned out to be anything but routine. They put him to work designing the latest and greatest in invisible body wear for Warrior Life's armed forces, instead of Uncle Sam's. These suits were as black as night, invisible to radar or infrared, waterproof, and odorless, meaning that the ten Warrior Life Duppy frogmen slithering under the main moat's gate and silently into the sewer system of the two-hundred-year-old fortress wouldn't smell of shit when they emerged into the fort's belly and made their way to the toilet ducts of each cell to free their respective targets.

G-Money knew how important it was for each liberator to greet his woman's face firsthand, both for her seeing him pop up from behind a toilet in the wall and because it was the smartest way to silently slip these women out of their chains in between guard counts in the middle of the night. Others stood in the shadows of strategic entry points, on cue, when garbage gates opened and food boats backed into the ports at the back of the fort, bringing the latest food loads aboard. Tonight, rather than using them as a load-in point, Daco had converted G-Money's fleet of rescue vessels—deep-sea submersibles capable of carrying up to sixteen passengers at a time—to drone-driven vessels to cut down on weight and add speed.

Docked underwater in the darkness, they waited mere feet away to surface and then submerge these prisoners to freedom. General Abbé stood on his balcony, several hundred feet above, staring out at the night sky, listening to the waves crash against his palace below. He had no idea this would be his final night in power. Silently, as guards slept at their stations, outside and inside, G-Money nodded at Daco, giving the green light to begin his latest video game from one hundred thousand leagues under the sea. Signals went off around the fortress, and the first infiltrations began. There would be no inside men on tonight's mission. G-Money couldn't trust any of these soon-to-be-shark-bait suckers. He watched the operation play out on thirty cameras around the castle as he took another deep hit of Jamaica's finest. He saw the black hood cover Abbé's head as the body harness was simultaneously attached, sending him sailing out to sea by parasail in the black of night. The needle he'd felt hit his neck as he was thrust into a wind tunnel would blunt the not-so-subtle slam his body would take into the side of the sub, as one of G-Money's most trusted Sistas delivered the general to a small drone that was waiting in the water as they landed two hundred meters offshore. They brought the general, bruised but alive and now in deep hibernation, to his ultimate fate as the drone submerged and delivered Abbé to G-Money.

Meanwhile, broken women huddled naked or nearly naked in rags in the corner of their filthy cells. Beds had been stripped of sheets, removing any sense of dignity. They dreamed of the last time they'd felt like humans, but those nightmares were suddenly interrupted. With wide eyes, they watched as toilets were pushed back from the walls, all in one simultaneous and synchronous action to cut down on noise. Most thought they were still dreaming as their husbands' faces and saving arms soon appeared. With silent hugs, most were pulled into the holes before they had time to cry out, while guard positions from around the fortress were stormed in the same few seconds.

Though twenty-six of the one hundred men from the Warrior Life extraction teams would die that night, they took 386 of the general's men with them and did so with valor that would have made their countries, fathers, wives, children, and fellow Warrior Life soljas proud.

G-Money wiped several tears from his eyes that night as he witnessed the liberation of seventy-three women by their husbands. These women had been enslaved into captivity and had given up questioning whether they'd be saved and by whom.

G-Money would groom these new families when he relocated them to carry on the Warrior Life movement for generations to come. His closest soljas had seen him cry before but never as a sign of weakness; rather, it was as permission to celebrate or mourn—a real man could kill and then cry about it. But far more tears of happiness were cried that night as eighteen Warrior Life drones emerged, rescuing and reuniting a total of 208 husbands and wives, sisters, brothers, and family members.

At the same time, those twenty Warrior Life Duppy Squad members who had enlisted for this mission, knowing they were facing certain death, had done it proudly, taking pride in the sight of the massacre of evil they had achieved. In a victory measured by body count, these were men who had been saved by G-Money from the streets and put on the battlefield again for one final victory, one final reminder of the soldiers they'd once been. Even with whatever injuries had sidelined them, G-Money had kept his personal promise to each to make them glorious again, and tonight's strike was their finest hour. They were not only liberating hundreds of innocent women and children but were effectively shutting down one of the leading exporters of child porn and sex trafficking in the Caribbean. They corralled the remaining soldiers from the general's rogue army into the main gladiator pit, which still sat as a tourist attraction at the center of the fort, where a giant movie screen, straight out of a Midtown Manhattan theater, now hung. Soon G-Money's face appeared to the captive audience of the worst of the general's army. G-Money had ordered they be kept alive for the demonstration of true power that would follow.

"Good evening, traitors, rapists, killers of innocents!" G-Money said from the screen. "You are on trial tonight, along with your leader. As you shared in his tyranny, now God Money will see you share in his fate!"

Daco then read a litany of charges, most already brought officially by UN tribunals that had been after the general for years. G-Money shook his head, listening. He had a separate screen that the general and he only could see together, and Abbé trembled as he watched, with G-Money's knife to his throat, the crying faces of his victims. At that moment, they could all see him too—they now were safely submerged below the sea in the arms of their husbands—and they could see the fear in his eyes for the first time. It was something G-Money had promised their Duppy husbands, and he reveled in this latest moment of history, salvation, and liberation that he was experiencing, along with his people, all as one. Everyone felt it like a current throughout the Warrior Life movement around the world, as they quietly rooted for G-Money's blade to cross the finish line. They listened as the charges continue to be read: one thousand counts of rape, twenty counts of murder of an infant under one month old—the general was a monster, the kind most people only met in movies or read about in history books. Tonight, the world would witness his execution, live.

G-Money's master stroke to the evening's entertainment was to have the general's body sacrificed, live on the Warrior Life TV network, going viral around the globe in real time. His crimes against humanity were read aloud as he performed a traditional wanga, the name for a voodoo blood-sacrifice ceremony. It was a spell he had cast with the helping hand of Haiti's oldest living witch doctor, the great-granddaughter of the legendary Marie Catherine Laveau, mother of modern voodoo. G-Money felt the moment of truth fill him and his people as he nodded to Daco. Warrior Life's team of hackers was soon busy, dancing away on their keyboards, hacking into and quickly taking over the comedy shows and news outlet broadcasts of the major television and streaming networks around the globe. Even G-Money's personal favorite network was hacked, the televisions in Times Square in the center of New York City, and would witness Abbé's execution. Why should he get the luxury of years of UN appeals, when swift justice could follow tonight, cleansing the souls of his victims in a single stroke of a knife.

With the swiftness of a pen signing a death warrant, G-Money gave his captive audience around the world what they wanted, relieving Abbé of his rank as he condemned the general to death with one slice of heavenly justice for all watching. Those who were already members of his movement became that much more fierce in their loyalty. Those who counted themselves new to the ranks had their reverence reinforced, and it made them stand at instant attention to the fact that G-Money and Warrior Life were no joke. As blood sprayed their screens like in a horror film, the general's head was quickly stuck to the appropriate stake and set afire to burn before the eyes of his watching victims. Such justice was rarely promised, let alone executed, with the expert efficiency G-Money and his Warrior Life team had done.

The next and final scene of the night that anyone would see from the viral version of the video, which would rack up 250 million views in the next twenty-four hours, was G-Money's personal message to his latest liberated: "You're free, Ma. You're with your man. Take hold of his arms like hope, and heal. You'll be home soon. Your only loyalty is to Warrior Life now, Ma, and you'll never be a prisoner again to anyone."

Watching his favorite circle of pet sharks eat the remains of the general as he basked in the sun coming up over the Caribbean, G-Money counted lucky stars as they faded from the safety of the night, knowing he'd soon have to submerge to his own cell. It was far prettier than for most prisoners, and he wasn't naive enough to think he ever could walk freely down the most anonymous street or country road or even dirt path from his past. He would always be hunted, always be feared, but as Pac had carried the word of Niccolò Machiavelli forward, he would also always be loved. Today, he embraced the hugs of hundreds of newly freed women like a hug from the warm morning sun. He took a long, last drag of his cigar-sized blunt and said goodbye to the sunlight. He knew, right then, that other faces were basking in it for the first time, as his fleet of drones delivered them to their promised shores, and Warrior Life lived on to fight another day for the people.

CHAPTER 9

WARRIOR LIFE FAMILY

G-MONEY HAD HIS EYES SQUARELY on the future. He'd seen the future ten years ago when OG Daco had first sold him on the importance of investing 25 percent of Warrior Life's annual revenues in cyber operations, from hacking to building out their cryptocurrency network; from bribes of the right low-level, woefully underpaid computer sectors who were ripe for the picking—some of Warrior Life's strongest early recruitments—to the kinds of technological investments in hacking and satellite infrastructure that only major governments like the US, Russia, and China had the budgets to sink their money at the time.

Within a decade, G-Money's cyber operations rivaled them all, world class and advancing, like James Cameron with *Avatar* or George Lucas with *Star Wars* back in the late '70s, when no one else would back his futuristic vision. G-Money was going sci-fi with this shit!

He knew his life wouldn't last forever, but he was ensuring his Warrior Life family would. The Kennedys had started out in bootlegging, and then went straight, and then straight to the top, all the way to the presidency. Even Michael Corleone had desired to go legitimate in *The Godfather* when he shifted the family's investments into legal gambling in Las Vegas. The difference was that G-Money didn't want to be president; he didn't want to take Warrior Life legitimate. Quite simply, he was happiest and most powerful in the shadows. Here, he could buy one country's law enforcement while another hunted him. He could play one drug cartel against another and battle one another to the death, while he quietly took control of their routes. Warrior Life prepared to take control of the financial side of organized crime by becoming its official bank.

Warrior Life had begun building to this position of power by laundering money for the cartels, American and Japanese Mafia, all into the safest cryptocurrency on the market. As his operation, supervised by OG Numbers and the Warrior Life team of the world's top hackers, everybody got richer, so everyone went along. That soon attracted those drug lords who weren't savages and wanted their own positions to grow stronger by keeping more of their washed money in safer places than banks, which could be seized by the US or their own crusading governments, and G-Money was happy to have their business.

Instead of getting tangled in legitimate business fronts, G-Money's Warrior Life money laundering agency was naturally attractive for criminals because, for a fee, they could wash the dirty money cleanly away into cyberspace, replacing it with completely legitimate digital assets. His network had pioneered this field's cutting edge, as well as keeping it sharper than law enforcement could ever keep up with or even have competitors. Those who tried to cut into Warrior Life's client market were quickly decapitated by a government seizure, leaked by the Warrior Life hacking squad. McNair had even gotten some G-Money leads to dismantling his financial networks, which resulted in money-laundering competitors actually being neutralized.

Today, G-Money was executing an operation that had been years in the making. Given the viral success several months back of his beheading of a traitor and then his son beheading his own mother for similar betrayals of Warrior Life, the fear factor was chilling any further thoughts of rebellion from among the routes and ranks of the criminal global underworld he currently controlled. He would expand that realm like Alexander or Caesar had done, just as Pac had envisioned decades earlier—total world domination, or as close to it as he could come. Quite simply, G-Money was about to reorganize the power structure of organized crime by becoming its bank, similar to the Joker in *The Dark Knight*, except there would be no money to set on fire. Instead, it would be converted to Warrior Life cryptocurrency and would make his organization invulnerable to betrayal because he could make their money disappear with the simple push of a button.

G-Money didn't steal; he didn't want more than he was entitled to have in commissions. He simply wanted to neutralize the threat of unnecessary rivalries getting in the way. To quote the great Nino Brown in *New Jack City*, "If they won't roll with us, we'll roll right over them!" G-Money wasn't a bully uprooting tradition as much as he was a bulldozer uprooting rotten foundations. He would, by the numbers, convince his soon-to-be partners that they had no choice but to adapt to his way. Adapt and survive—it was a simple message, one that drove nature and big business. Ultimately, even if he had to muscle his way in, G-Money's deal was an offer—as the Corleones said—that none of his competitors could afford to refuse.

The next generation of leaders of these crime families and organizations knew this too, and it was their job to help sell their elder bosses on that fact. G-Money had privately made deals with each of these consiglieres, underbosses, captains, assistants, and other protégés who needed an incentive to see that they would be dealing with him anyway, when they were in charge themselves in the years to come.

Much like displaced factory workers having to learn a new trade to be competitive in today's technologically driven world, mid-level lieutenants in the trades of organized crime were expected to be good on the streets with the traditional collection and gambling rackets that brought in the weekly takes they kicked up to their bosses but also to become savvy with computers, as more and more of gambling was becoming an online business. Similar to a stock scam, the best and brightest rose through the ranks, and now sat with their elder Mafia bosses, squabbling about how to operate increasingly sophisticated black market smartphones. They offered reassurances that they only half believed about the phones being untraceable, due to "this nerd" or "that geek" on the payroll who scrambled cell signals. Their favorite was, "What is Facetime? Is the call being videoed? Could it be used in a court proceeding if the government got a copy without a warrant?"

They were right to be cautious, even as they were forced into a brave new unknown world of cyber-driven organized crime. All these bosses, whether yelling at their subordinates in Japanese or a thick Brooklyn Italian accent, knew the percentages of their takes came, increasingly, courtesy of cyber crimes, from online credit card fraud to digital stock pump-and-dump operations to the recent national legalization of online gambling.

If customers didn't pay, they still got a visit from Moose and Rocco to physically give up the money, one way or another. A broken finger or arm was still a broken arm, but now, with the education on cryptocurrency that they were all being forced to undertake, there was a clear opening for someone with the same position and interests who could explain and make it simple for them to understand.

That was where G-Money stepped in. Warrior Life would make it as simple as the Mafia had whenever someone owed money and didn't pay: their options were limited. For the rapidly shifting global status of currencies, which rose and fell with the frequency and uncertainty of the NASDAQ, Warrior Life cryptocurrency was as reliable and safe as US government bonds. Organized crime's money-laundering operations, for the first time in their centuries-long history, would be completely insulated from seizure. It was that simple.

They would make deposits as regularly as a normal citizen did every day in their FDIC-secured bank, and Warrior Life guaranteed every dollar they washed. That was the brilliance of G-Money's operation. Anyone who dared steal from him was stealing from the most feared crime lords and organizations on earth, giving everyone involved in the illegal activity a common interest in staying honest. Vigilantes who might rob a diamond dealer were less likely to do so now, according to the statistics that G-Money would show these Mob bosses, relative to the past ten years, as Warrior Life took over more and more illegal revenue routes around the globe, either through force or partnership, from diamond routes to drug smuggling.

Everyone's product was arriving safer, with fewer deaths and greater profits around the world for all parties involved. One of the most powerful stats that G-Money would break out in today's presentation was the record plummet in government seizures of illegal currencies and product around the globe. From narcotics to diamonds to every other racket that had long allowed organized crime to exist and thrive, the Warrior Life take-over had made everyone more money, and that was always the bottom line: *how much more money can we make?* G-Money would happily tell them, and it was in the trillions.

The best part was that Warrior Life's commission would be the same across the spectrum of services they provided within their money-laundering operation. Whether washing newly collected monies from a drug transaction or laundering one of the hundreds of corrupt government officials they employed around the world, Warrior Life guaranteed every dollar, under punishment of beheading. G-Money didn't fuck around with torture; he went straight for the throat. Nothing scared even the scariest gangster more than the thought of having his head chopped off with a machete. G-Money had already provided all the visual proof they needed to know he wasn't to be fucked with. Nobody stole from Warrior Life, and under the organization's protection, these mobsters and criminal organizations could sleep better at night, knowing no one would fuck with their money either.

Guys still got arrested, but they'd have even more money now, as well as an easier way to go about it, to bribe the necessary law enforcement officials they needed to free their key guys. The bottom line was that Warrior Life was now their bank, whether they wanted to go along with that or not. Those who didn't would be even more vulnerable to government asset seizures because they would now be exposed, devoid of the protection that G-Money's world-class hacking infrastructure offered. It had proven impenetrable so far; in fact, another stat G-Money would boast about was his organization's recruiting record for the world's top hackers. Where many used to flip on their illegal employers and go to work for the government to avoid prison, most now worked for G-Money. Those who didn't were sitting in a cell somewhere, being ass-raped, with no chance at parole or even touching a computer keyboard for decades to come. G-Money controlled enough of the legal apparatuses of the governments that prosecuted the hackers who wouldn't go to work for Warrior Life to make an example out of them, and that was even harsher than anything the legal authorities had to throw at them.

That kind of pressure had pushed every reluctant party to the table, and now they waited for the signal to broadcast for the encrypted cyber channel from which G-Money's conference call would commence, a satellite flying through space as he thought. In a few minutes, through some clever key stroking and ghosting from detection on US government radar, on the ground or in space, a twenty-minute meeting between the top organized crime families and organizations around the world would occur, one that rivaled the 1960s Mob meeting in upstate New York or the one in *The Godfather* movie, following the death of Santino Corleone.

Today, G-Money would make clear that he was sitting at the head of the table, and going into the future, he would be the equivalent of the United States in the United Nations. G-Money was reorganizing the illegal trades to make them less violent and more profitable. Ultimately, with the drop in body count and rise in yearly takes, arguably the most powerful statistic he would pull out on his underworld brethren today, they all stood to see a 20 percent across-the-board increase in profits under Warrior Life's cyber banking tutelage, between laundering and investment, for those who chose to take their partnerships further, based on those projections. Everything G-Money had set in motion when he'd first gone on the run was now coming to fruition.

It was a new reality that made for a brave new world, as well as one that Warrior Life would shape in its own message, culture, code, creed, colors, vision, and, ultimately, legacy. The Bloods and the Crips would be his hardest targets to tame, and he was saving that street battle for another day. Today, G-Money would send a loud-and-clear message: *Warrior Life bleeds green.* These Mob bosses would get their money, but G-Money knew as well as any of these bosses that it ultimately was not just about the guys at the top but the guys on the street, equally, and with his grassroots efforts, that would ultimately be the biggest sell.

Countries in Africa were so poor that villages didn't even have running water, but the billion dollars that Warrior Life had privately spent to irrigate the African continent, across the Congo and the Kalahari and Sahara Deserts, had instantly bought the loyalty of the people. Warrior Life had spent hundreds of millions eliminating corruption by sending in its armed forces to guard construction budgets and contracts. The real peasants of the war-torn territories, the urban jungles of Libya, had been paid revolutionary wages to rebuild those cities and neighborhoods with state-of-the-art digital infrastructure for high-speed internet and modernized apartment complexes, with state-of-the-art appliances and free energy bills. G-Money had strengthened that loyalty by keeping the construction jobs loyal. Soon, he controlled their unions, making governments poorer by contract and modernizing the third world's biggest continent in under a decade, to be competitive with South America and fast gaining on Europe.

It cost the local governments nothing and made their people so happy that protests and outright rebellions stopped overnight. Warrior Life had subsidized the taxes and kick-backs so everyone—to quote the late, great Biggie Smalls—"was living better now!" G-Money sat atop it all, this among his crowning moments, a throne invisible but feared enough that his Warrior Life kingdom would reign supreme forever.

He was taking his seat at the table today, whether he was welcome or not. It was a power play, for sure, but one that would seem so welcome and inevitable at the end of his presentation that he was almost assured of victory. As an insurance policy, anyone who bucked would have half their year's profit margin erased with the stroke of a few keys and replaced, minus Warrior Life's commission and a guarantee of future cooperation. He knew he couldn't just behead the boss of the Gambino crime family, but G-Money had those bitches in checkmate, and he knew it. Soon, they would know it too, but his strike had to hit much harder and less savagely, right in the heart of the motivation that drove illegal crime most: *money*. Warrior Life was about to become the bank.

As his eyes opened, G-Money's black mask was pulled tautly over his face. His eyes were the only thing his new business partners would see and the only thing they needed to focus on, along with, of course, the Fortune 500 shit corporate presentation he was about to drop on them. "Daco, pull the curtain up on these motherfuckers!" he said. "Let's show them who is the new Oz of this shit!"

OG Daco spoke a few words and launched a concerto of keyboards typing in perfect harmony. His thirty-screen operation room suddenly was populated with faces of all ethnic origins and age ranges, from the youngest bosses among them, in their early and mid-forties, to those who'd reigned over their families and territories for decades, in their mid-seventies and even some who were older. Both of those were Asian crime lords. It intrigued G-Money, in a private moment of observation regarding their health and culture, that through cleaner living, a longer rule was possible versus the hard-partying appetites of some of his company that plainly showed on their faces. G-Money could see that some had vicious hangovers, while the active coke habits of others were obvious in their early-morning jitters. They knew they needed to be sober for this meeting, and G-Money would soon show them why.

"Good morning, comrades around the world! G-Money, Warrior Life boss, coming to you this morning. I thought it was time we all finally met face-to-face. I got some numbers to break out on y'all, and then I'll take some questions. I think you'll find, at the end of the conversation, that it is, to quote Michael Corleone, an offer you'll find hard to refuse!"

Don Scungilli, head of the Queens crime family that bore his name, nearly cut G-Money off as he spoke up. "Who the fuck is this guy to tell me how to wash my money? I want to know that. Why shouldn't I just cut your head off right now? I hear you banana boys like that!"

"I got an answer for that question right now," G-Money quickly retorted. "Watch the screen in front of you that your much-more-capable subordinate set up. That should clear it up for you. As your people have shown you through various channels inside and outside of your immediate realm, where your family's money is cleaned globally, Warrior Life cryptocurrency presently washes 70 percent of your family's dirty money clean. The present value, as you can see, for this year's profit is $89 million—up 20 percent since we started handling your account two years ago. Had you been smart enough to stay with us, it would likely rise another 20 percent to over $100 million before the year is out. Now, you'll top out at half that—$50 million!"

Don Scungilli's eyes widened and veins exploded from his neck in anger as his consigliere quickly whispered in his ear, trying to calm him down.

G-Money saw it as the perfect opportunity to cut in and seal the deal, "Now it's $50 million. Any other questions, comrades? G-Money's got the floor now. I'mma lay it all out for you ..."

By the time he was done, the expressions on everyone's faces had changed from varying scowls and shock to calm resignation and, in some cases, smiles. G-Money's numbers had been impressive, and his lesson on how quickly those numbers could change, one way or another, made even more of an impression. They all knew he was the man now, and even while some would call him all manner of racial slurs in the rants that followed at the end of the call, they all knew their money was safer with Warrior Life as their new full-time banker.

It had been a great success for those seconds-in-command who had shepherded their aging bosses through the decision process with periodic ear whispers. Even before the call was disconnected, several checked silent cell phone messages that alerted them to the $2 million a piece in bonuses that had arrived in their numbered WL crypto accounts. G-Money's cyber shit was safer than Switzerland! G-Money was building the first great twenty-first century crime family.

CHAPTER 10

REVOLUTIONARY ON RECORD

G-MONEY SAT IN THE VOCAL booth of his state-of-the-art recording studio, recording music at the bottom of the ocean. He would soon be the first leader of a socio-political movement to record and release his own soundtrack album, and, in trend with the catch-them-off-guard surprise albums that Drake, Beyonce, and Eminem had had such success with in the modern day of streaming music, G-Money would drop his own debut on the same day the Warrior Life flag unfurled for the first time. Thanks to both his street cred and the digital age of encrypted email, G-Money was rapping over beats from the hottest producers in hip-hop, everyone from Dr. Dre, Boi-1da, No I.D., and DJ Khaled to an international Who's Who that featured Salaam Remi, Alex da Kid, and Akon, to legends of the game like Pete Rock, Eric B., Easy Mo Bee, Sir Mix-a-Lot, the late, great Johnny "J," and others.

Tonight, he was working on a beat that the late Pac producer Johnny "J" had made for G-Money's mentor on the night he died. It had never been heard by the public—the Warrior Life anthem.

"Warrior Life Theme"
—God-Money
Droppin' million-dollar cash-loads on you assholes
Tryin' to take me down for ten years
On the run, now let's fast forward
To this time and space
This rhyme and place

Where my government's lovin' it
The way we reign down a new covenant
Where you have access like you never did before
Kids in Africa no longer growin' up poor
G-Money pimpin' with my face on the walls
Of abandoned buildings 'round the world, it's not so small
The following Warrior Life is hollowing
Out you playa hatas' fanbases, you'll soon be following
The same melody line all you other suckas do
Motherfuckers who, used to think you run shit—you're through

'Cause G-Money's takin' over
Like Caesar, Capone, or Gambino
Some shot-caller in Chino
I know all of these folks
Who you repress and keep down
They're risin' up now
Flyin' under the Warrior Life flag
With bombs 'n' calm both rainin' down

Round the world, G-Money's on fire
On the mic, smokin' like four Ferrari tires
Takin' off with the cops always behind me
FBI Top 10, but they never find me
Suckas, motherfuckers, I've got a growin' family
And you bitch-ass tricks'll never jam me
Up, 'cause I don't give a fuck
I'll blow your pussy asses up from a satellite in your truck
With missiles that leave a crater like one on the moon
I'm your nightmare, you're hell, you're temple of doom
Boom! Did you hear that blast
Is it a bomb or a speaker; Warrior Life will last
For ages, and pages of historical study
Enough books to fill a library, buddy
You better back up, or get smacked up, the new Pac
All respect to Run DMC, but I'm the new king of rock!

'Cause G-Money's got his name 'n' face on a C-note
Takin' over like Caesar, Capone, or Gambino,
Even some shot-caller in Chino
Trust me, dog; I'm tight w' all of these folks
Who you repress and keep down
Like Mandela but they're risin' up now
Flyin' under the Warrior Life flag
With bombs 'n' calm both rainin' down

His female engineers were cumming and starting to manage by the time G-Money finished dropping his dopest anthem yet. This was on some Ice Cube *AmeriKKKa's Most Wanted* shit, and by the time he was done, he would have an album's worth of pussy powder for his hoes! G-Money had groupies on stand-by, but he could trust each of them with his life, and with the orgy starting to take place as he called up the next instrumental track by phone order, G-Money knew he had a number-one album on his hands. He'd always known that penetrating the speakers of the homies on the corners around the world was the key to solidifying his reign over the streets, and this album would do it.

He'd drop the album and corresponding X-rated videos on the same day, flooding the porn sites, like Redtube and Pornhub, with the latest and greatest in Warrior Life porn, now among the most-streamed porn videos online, making G-Money one of the top porn stars in the world, even though it had been by happy accident.

Rather than the usual cheesy porn music, bitches all over the would be riding wood to G-Money's voice, and at the same time, he was bringing true his lifetime dream of being a multi-platinum recording artist and rap star. He knew he was Cube's descendant, and with this album, he would take over the beats in the streets and the game in the same time! G-Money was about to become the biggest outlaw and rap star in the world, a perfect synergy and realization of his initial Pac vision!

G-Money would always be a disciple of Pac, like Christ had been of God, or Malcolm X coming from Elijah Muhammad, Mike Tyson from Cus D'Amato, or John Gotti from Neil Dellacroce. By this point, G-Money had assumed the same role and had as many disciples of his own. Who would stand out would be determined first on this record, as he'd put the word out to millions of Warrior Life citizens that they could submit demos for it versus being considered for his upcoming album. Not only had it helped spread the word and the hype on streets around the world for G-Money's debut album—ten years in the making—but he was putting a billion-dollar marketing campaign into effect for free. G-Money knew the value of the dollar on wax, and he was about to become the Scarface or Donald Trump of the shit! Ice Cube was like one of the four faces on Mount Rushmore, and in hip-hop terms, that mountain would include Cube, Eminem, Pac, and G-Money!

He already had the redesign under way; it would take place by laser from satellite, implementing the latest power of his team's hacking capabilities, to redesign a mountain with a simple stroke of a few keys. History would be redesigned. Rakim's face probably would have been there in place of G-Money's, had his Caesar-like takeover not occurred. G-Money had already decided on that great historical ruler as his alter-ego moniker, like Pac had with "Makaveli." Julius Caesar, at the height of his power, controlled the Roman Empire, and as leader of the Warrior Life movement, G-Money controlled prop governments around the globe, from local to federal levels and every variation in between, depending on whether it was Africa or tribal Middle Eastern turf.

The bottom line was that his movement needed a theme song, and his people needed a soundtrack, and G-Money was about to give a double album of anthems, just like Pac had on *All Eyez on Me*.

As he finished laying his vocal double in tribute to Pac's signature vocal recording style, G-Money had Daco bring up the Boi-1da beat he'd been tripping off since he first heard it. He was about to bring it to life lyrically, and the topic was his favorite kind of Slick Rick-esque storytelling, about a ten-year rivalry between the hunter and the hunted, between Ryan Hardy and Joe Carroll, Elliott Ness and Al Capone, McNair and G-Money. Right there, he titled the track, "Ness vs. Capone."

> Poor Agent McNair, he used to have hair
> First it went gray, then gone
> Chasin' G-Money the past ten years
> Jeez, has it been that long?
> And what's taking you so long to catch the fox
> So frustrated by now you must be smokin' rocks

To deal with the constant embarrassment and humiliation
Downstairs in your musty, depressing basement
Where my mug shot's been on the wall collecting dust
For longer than you been on your knees jugglin' deez nuts
God-Money, I'm representin' Warrior Life
While you're out chasin' me, I'm in your bed makin' a whore of your wife
That video's goin' live on all kinds of porno sites
Unless you resign tonight, you're washed up, not fit for the fight

G-Money bitch, smackin' all you law enforcement hoes
Huntin' me all over the world, but you're not even close
For all you know, I'm floatin' 'round up in space
One thing I do know, WL straight jizzin' all over y'all's face

From N.W.A.'s "Fuck tha Police," "911 Is a Joke" by P. E.
"Crooked Officer" by the Geto Boys, "Cop Killer" by Ice-T
Bob Marley "Shot the Sheriff" in self-defense
G-Money gunnin' too after so many assassination attempts
By the powers that be, tryin' to keep a G down
You couldn't do it to Pac, won't do it to me now
I'm the new revolution, you're the old solution
I see your ass, on site, swear to Makaveli I'm shootin'
Lootin' your banks, fuckin' your skanks, makin' you my hoes
Fuckin' with G-Money, that's just how it goes 'n' goes
On 'n' on, Warrior Life pimpin' your asses like Dolomite
Liberace meets Kadafi, that's what I'm rollin' like
With bling on my rings alone that would outshine a king's
Crown, bow down, 'n' listen to my bitches sing

G-Money bitch, smackin' all you law enforcement hoes
Huntin' me all over the world but you're not even close
For all you know, I'm floatin' 'round up in space
One thing I do know, WL straight jizzin' all over y'all's face

Rapping over the classic "My Ambitionz Az a Ridah" beat that Daz
had produced for Pac had opened the now legendary *All Eyez on Me* album.

G-Money, rather than rapping over Pac's sacred track, preferred a spoken word vibe to his latest proverb to his people. Every G-Money preaching was set to music. Where preaching was involved, he'd always felt his people better tuned in to his words with music, and because Pac was Warrior Life's spiritual leader, the equivalent of its Bob Marley, G-Money wanted to continue proudly in that tradition with his debut LP. He would be dropping dozens of albums, like Pac had, in the years to come, but he knew nothing beat the debut LP—it was the first impression, and he didn't want his people liking the album out of fear but rather love for his Makaveli-inspired style and sound. Cueing up the track, G-Money put on his $400,000 Chopard sunglasses, took in a half-inch drag off a cigar-sized joint, and began dropping science for his people over the classic beat.

Soul Ridah

Soul Ridah
Warrior Life fighter
Loyal to G-Money
Fightin' for a new country
Power without borders
All runnin' on my orders
And as we're movin' forward
All y'all bitches' reigns gettin' shorter
Cause I'm freedom's no. 1 importer
to places that before were
under power-hungry rule
I'm like Daenerys w' the unsullied fool
All follow me because they choose
I'm mackin' with a dragon hot as my AK shoots
Ride or die like Pac so we just can't lose

'Cause I'm a Soul Ridah
Warrior Life fighter
Livin' a Thug Life, the rough type
Fuck w' G 'n' I'll drop you on sight

For years without fear, been the no. 1 shot-caller
Like a bare-knuckles cage fighter, straight baller
Hauler of mo' cash in bags than the biggest street boss
Rollin' over yo' Hummer w' my tanks as I floss
Round the world, pick up your girl right off your arm
Whether on the corner or out on the weed farm
I like 'em young, fresh 'n' green like Biggie
But best believe G-Money's got some cougars rollin' w' me
Bitches of every nationality, acknowledge G
As they baby-daddy-to-be, if they win the lottery
Power ball, holler y'all, 'cause now ya down with tha king!
Like Run DMC or Schoolly D-PSK "What Does It Mean?"
Makin' green, naked scene, never workin' again
Come on, girl, I'll take you to that spiritual Zen

'Cause I'm a Soul Ridah
Warrior Life fighter
Livin' a Thug Life, the rough type
Fuck w' G 'n' I'll drop you on sight

"Yo, Daco," G-Money called out. "You got that IllaDaProducer beat, that kid who did Eminem's *Kamikaze* beat? I'm feelin' like bombin' on these bitches with somethin' hard! Pull the track up. Let's call this one 'Commando'!"

Eminem had "Venom" on *Kamikaze*
Now I'm in the hot seat, murderin' paparazzi
Or anyone tryin' to take my picture
G-Money's like Skynet, the way he hits ya
Like a mushroom cloud when I punch you out
like Tyson bitch, one hit'll shut ya down
round after round blastin' out my mouth
got a hot pen like Rakim, like Big, I now wear a crown
not the king of New York, but the king of the world
motherfuck Leo, I'm *Titanic*, volcanic, the wind in a whirl
fast as my tongue spits, just like a tommy gun

the way I fuck around on the mic, John Dillinger son
killin' the fun when it's time to get down to business
The new Caesar, time for y'all to bear witness

'Cause I'm M-60 strong like Rambo
Takin' out 100 motherfuckers like *Commando*
Schwarzenegger in *Predator*, got so much ammo
I might as well have my own action film channel!

Got an alphabet soup of guns to pull on your troops
From AKs to 9mms along with the stomp of a million boots
Times two, all marchin' 'n' chargin' on G-Money's green light
Even from 10,000 miles away, I got your ass in my sights
With one push of a button from a satellite
Or in a rage on stage, tearin' you up w' my battle mic
Back in the days growin' up in BK, the NYC
G-Money bitch, trust you ain't never seen a G like me
Warrior Life, backed up by millions around the globe
G-Money, rappin' in combat boots, boxers 'n' a silk king's robe
At 3 a.m. in the vocal booth, proof that I'm rollin' like Pac
24/7, never stop, round the clock, always on lock, ready to drop
The next verse, or worse, a missile on your little bitch ass
So bob your head, or bow down 'n' get ready for the whiplash

'Cause I'm M-60 strong like Rambo
Takin' out 100 motherfuckers like *Commando*
Schwarzenegger in *Predator*, got so much ammo
I might as well have my own action film channel!

Out of breath, like a boxer after twelve rounds, he dominated yet again on the lyrical battlefield with the second verse of "Commando." G-Money took another deep drag off a blunt and pulled a 40 of Colt .45 out of his vocal booth fridge, where he kept a literal variety store's worth of different beverages to suit every song, mood, or occasion, where inspiration ordered a different drink than the previous song had. Switching from bottled water to Billy D. Williams's and Brooklyn's favorite 40 ounce, he took a long swig as

Daco pulled up a never-before-heard beat from RZA. G-Money was about to ride over a Wu-Tang Clan beat and couldn't believe he was about to join the ranks of Method Man, Ol' Dirty Bastard, Ghostface Killah, and on and on in the proud lineage of Wu-Tang, now counting Warrior Life as part of the clan. Hearing the hypnotic beat fill his headphones, G-Money closed his eyes and began to float into the vibe of the dream beat.

Deep

Just like the sub-bass thumpin' in your Jeep
Bumpin' G-Money while you're rollin' down the street
I'm on some other level shit like the Scarface, Bushwick, 'n' Willie D
Tryin' to fuck with this Geto B? Don't be silly, G!
My first entry into the hip-hop century
'n' already changin' the game fundamentally
both instrumentally 'n' lyrically, let's keep it real, G
Only Warrior Life's got this kind of artillery
It's thrillin' me, but there's so much you're still to see
As G-Money reveals shit like Merlin, Houdini, or Copperfield
Though it may look like an optical illusion, I'm for real
just like my DJ on the turntable wheels
or like I am in the streets when I'm blastin' the steel

I guess sometimes a thought was meant to be
Go 'head 'n' try to turn a deaf ear to my creed
Warrior Life philosophy hottest on the street
Could there be a deeper emcee out there? Not possibly!

From Bob Marley all the way back to Socrates
All these heavy motherfuckers with different philosophies
Makaveli, brought full circle by Pac
Back in the day, but you know the shit never stops
I mix 'em all up like playas on a chess board
But G-Money's droppin' science, 'bout to be the next Lord
The Bobby Fischer of the shit, all the chin strokers on my dick
Warrior Life's a bible, not just some motherfuckin' manuscript

'n' all y'all followas who had a subscription, canceled quick
As soon as they heard G-Money on the mic
Now they overnight disciples lickin' honey off the pipe
Buzzin' like bumble bees, y'all dumb emcees better never come at me
'cause all the brothas in the streets sayin', "Damn that G-Money's deep!"

I guess sometimes a thought was meant to be
Go 'head 'n' try to turn a deaf ear to my creed
Warrior Life philosophy hottest on the street
Could there be a deeper emcee out there? Not possibly!

Done dropping science for the moment, G-Money opened up his math book on these fools as he looked at the first proof of the official Warrior Life currency with G-Money's face printed on every bill. He'd drop millions of these from the air around the world before shit was over, and he was about to drop the ultra-smack down on those cash-flashin' hoes trying to rock it like their gold necklaces and watches weren't rented. As they said in *Alpha Dog*, "The only thing these guys are shooting is music videos, dog!"

G-Money was about to clear the fog; make these bitches fear the dog. Laughing, he could see his mind was already rapping on the track. He had Daco throw on a smooth No I.D. track straight from his Jay Z vault. It was G-Money's turn to take Wall Street by storm.

Wall Street

Goin' back retro on some Gordon Gekko–type shit
G-Money's clip fatter than a blimp or a pimp's
Bankroll, and I throw them 'round like baseball
Right in they face y'all, G-Money erase y'all
Names off the Forbes or Fortune richest list
'Cause my stacks of cash like the Joker in bliss
In *The Dark Knight*, settin' fire to mob money
But fuckin' with mine, that shit is not funny
It'll earn you a price on your head you'll never dodge
Lil Shorties sayin', "Damn, G-Money's livin' large!"
from jimmy size to winning prize, Warrior Life's a conglomerate

straight up dominant, a fuckin' poet like Vonnegut
the most you gonna get is run out of the business
so step the fuck off while G-Money rip this

I'm Charlie Sheen in *Wall Street*
Drownin' in millions, G-Money's balls deep
On some Bill Gates/Warren Buffett shit
Got my face on my own $100 bills, bitch!

This is G-Money's call to all you hoes
in all fours, lined up outside my bedroom door
I'm gonna run a train like Vince Neil in Motley
through all you girls, girls, girls with the hottie bodies
G-Money just takin y'all Warrior Life explorers
way past Dora, on a tour-a
my own private marijuana forest
where every tree has phosphorous

Science class shit, stickin' up for the ganja saga
of that new weed movement, G-Money is the fatha
the kind stuff, high up like a king on a throne
Jordan in the zone, sittin' at the top of the Dow Jones
Keep growin' higher and higher with the green
Dollars 'n' weed, diamonds 'n' G's Warrior Life settin' ya free

I'm Charlie Sheen in *Wall Street*
Drownin' in millions, G-Money's balls deep
On some Bill Gates/Warren Buffett shit
Got my face on my own $100 bills, bitch!

As G-Money wrapped his last vocal of the night, his voice shredded, out of breath, like he'd been running a marathon, he knew he'd left it all on the field or on the track. He knew that gangstas around the world would be ridin' to his records; putting in work to his beats on the streets. NFL and NBA players would be working out to his jams before games. Soljas would be bumpin' his shit in tanks and Humvees as they fought wars on the battlefields around the world. Convicts would work out in the yard with

G-Money blasting out of the boom boxes. Activists would march with his songs as their theme music around the world. And there would be lots of parades and celebrations too! Shit, a new generation of Warrior Life babies would be conceived as Gs rocked their girls to his rhythms and lyrics, including more members of G-Money's own tribe. This was the Warrior Life soundtrack to a revolutionary on record, and if they broke enough records, he'd become the first true *gangster* rapper, street solja, and outlaw on the run to crack number one on the Billboard Top 200 Albums chart!

CHAPTER 11

WARRIOR LIFE ILLUMINATI

THE TERM *ILLUMINATI* REFERRED TO a secret society, dating back historically to a sixteenth-century sect of Spanish heretics who claimed extraordinary spiritual enlightenment. The next iteration came a hundred years later, in 1776, when Adam Weishaupt founded Bavarian Illuminati, which was then carried on by the Free Masons, the most prominent US secret society, with founding members like George Washington, Benjamin Franklin, and John Hancock. More recently, the Bilderberg group allegedly ran the twentieth-century version of the same club, founded by Prince Bernhard of the Netherlands, with the design in mind to align the global interests, financial and otherwise, of the United States and Europe, where conspiracy theorists argued a new world order.

Secret societies followed through the ages, both rumored and confirmed, dramatized in books, film, television, and, finally, the internet, where the conspiracies raged, typically among the less-educated, blue-collar classes around the world about master-of-the-universe societies like these that ran everything, even political systems, where elections were essentially meaningless because the people weren't choosing their leader, or if they were, it was by force.

From the Mafia in the US tossing the 1960 presidential election to Kennedy through their control of the labor unions and who their members voted for, to North Korean dictator Kim Jong-un's "democratic" elections, where he ran unopposed with almost 100 percent of the vote in his favor, G-Money had watched the fortunate sons have their run for decades—shit, for centuries!

G-Money already had started shifting the balance in power around the globe. In the third-world countries that G-Money had helped to free in recent years, where dictatorships had ruled and reigned, there was, no doubt, credence behind this belief among the peasant populations that they had no choice but to vote for whoever had a gun pointed at their heads. G-Money had liberated many of these people, most prolifically across the African continent and third world, but he'd had equal success in the urban centers he controlled around the globe, taking the power away from the elites and returning it to the streets, just as Pac had prophesized during Thug Life that his people would one day.

Pac himself had revealed before his death that the *Makaveli* album was Pac

> enforcing my mind strength. That's what's more important to me that people see now, that this wasn't no accident, I plotted every single step—from this to this. Niggas was telling me about the Illuminati shit while I was in jail, and I'm putting a K in it because I'm killing that Illuminati shit! By the next election, I *promise* you I'm going to be sitting across from all the Presidents. I'm going to be so far from where I am now, four years, God-willing I'm alive, I guarantee you we *will* have our own political party. And it won't just be for black people, it will be for Mexicans, I don't give a fuck, all you lost-tribe motherfuckers right now, we need to have our own political party ... I go down paths that haven't been traveled before.

He had been on the way to forming his own street Illuminati, kicking his new movement off with the final studio album he recorded before his death, *The Don Killuminati: The 7 Day Theory*, under the moniker Makaveli, a clever play on Niccolò Machiavelli, who, as author of *The Prince*, remains arguably the greatest war strategist, next to Sun Tzu with the equally influential *The Art of War*.

G-Money had read both books hundreds of times over and had studied every word as he'd spent the past decade outlining the chapters of his own *Warrior Life Illuminati* manuscript. With a twenty-first-century edition of both of the latter texts, G-Money's would be studied by scholars for centuries to come, both on earth and beyond, in cyberspace, song, literature—shit, they would be teaching courses at Ivy League universities on *Warrior Life Illuminati* one hundred years from now!

Rolling Stone magazine had agreed and eloquently argued:

> No other rapper has generated a legend as profound as *The Don Killuminati: The Seven Day Theory*, the 1996 album that fueled widespread belief that he had somehow survived the Las Vegas shooting. There was speculation that Pac called himself Makaveli to evade his antagonists, much as the political theorist Niccolo Machiavelli had claimed to do in The Prince five centuries earlier. *The Seven Day Theory* is modeled on Machiavelli's claim that he faked death for seven days; Shakur was pronounced dead six days after being shot. As an argument that Shakur is chilling on an island somewhere, it's suspect. As an incredible piece of myth-making, it has no equal in the genre.

"No equal"—until now. G-Money would never be Pac's equal, but he was considered by his people to be the equivalent of a son, like Jesus to God, or Bob Marley. He'd begun laying the groundwork for his own generation a decade ago. Ten years to the day, G-Money had started his own secret society, known as the Warrior Life Illuminati. He was a product of Pac's famed quote, "I may not change the world, but I bet I spark the brain that does change the world." G-Money was that mind, that offspring, who would carry the torch with a new age of enlightenment, one that would hold up to scrutiny from the best scholars and critics from every culture. Warrior Life's words would become a new bible for his people, and in preparation, G-Money had spent hours at the bottom of the ocean over the past decade, studying Pac like a monk studied scriptures.

He had a library with every known piece of writing on Pac, an archive of every magazine and video interview he'd ever given during his life, and he had almost become a historian on the subject of Pac's legend and legacy. Without question, it was the largest and most complete library on Pac in the world, and it belonged in the National Archives in Washington, DC.

Still, G-Money liked having it all to himself. It was not just his study but his sanctuary, with walls decorated by the rarest and most expensive of Pac memorabilia from around the world, acquired on both the legitimate collector circuits and the black market.

As a gift for breaking him out of jail, Suge had given G-Money perhaps one of the most sought-after Pac collectables on the market, the actual death row medallion that Suge had given Pac upon his release from Clinton Correctional Facility and the one he wore twenty-four hours a day, through the very night of his assassination. Suge had taken it off Pac's neck on the way to the hospital to make sure no one would steal it, and he had held onto it since. Worth well over $15 million, at last check with the world's leading memorabilia experts, it hung encased in bullet-proof glass behind G-Money's desk in this very study.

He sat there for several helpless moments, staring, as a fan, at the treasured artifacts of his mentor, from his Rolls-Royce license plates—3RQS301, which G-Money had turned into one of Warrior Life's best-selling T-shirts—to the now-legendary handwritten contract that David Kenner had drafted at Clinton Correctional Facility that Pac and Suge both signed, guaranteeing his release and the recording revolution that followed.

In another frame, he had the handwritten lyrics to "California Love," a gold record from Thug Life, and even the BMW emblem from the car in which he and Suge had been shot on the night Pac had died. G-Money's children weren't even allowed to play in that room of the submarine; in fact, it was designed as an escape pod that could withstand a blast from ten of any of the world's top sub-busting missiles, and once it reached the surface, it would remain invisible to radar for a ten-thousand-mile radius, both on the surface of the ocean and when submerged. G-Money could live in that room for months, if needed. It was designed to preserve his Pac archive as a museum of sorts and could even be launched into space, if necessary, like a satellite, if he was on the run and had to abandon ship.

Still, he had no such plans or worries, as thanks to the advent of technology, G-Money would plant his *Warrior Life Illuminati* doctrine, from the bottom of the sea, onto every smartphone around the globe, from every major service provider, from Sprint to Asia Cell and every network in between.

By way of a new brilliant virus developed by Daco and his team, they would simply hack into billions of user profiles and plant the book in app form. It would simply open once a user clicked on it, providing not only an e-book version and personally narrated audio book versions of the *Warrior Life Illuminati* but the *Warrior Life* soundtrack album as well, along with other bonus content designed to create a ready-made solja out of anyone who wanted to enlist upon first listen.

G-Money didn't want disciples; he wanted Black Panthers, Nation of Islam, that kind of loyalty and allegiance, while still feeling freedom in the loyalty his soljas showed to Warrior Life. It was a volunteer army, and not everybody was picking up a fire arm. Some were weaponized with their minds, their keystrokes online, their social media freedom of speech, and, most importantly, their liberation from whatever previous prison to which they'd been sentenced, whether economic, religious, social, or military. G-Money was freeing every mind he could, just as Pac had, with the sound theory that they would follow his lead because it kept them from becoming slaves to the system. Everybody did better financially anyway, even the government officials he had to bribe. That was the cost of doing business, but G-Money had just as many spies within governments around the world, at every level, out of sheer loyalty to the cause and creed.

G-Money sat down to review his encrypted final draft of the *Warrior Life Illuminati* introduction before sending it to Daco for uploading into the master manuscript that would soon top every best-seller and streaming list around the world, whether the establishment wanted to acknowledge the numbers or not, officially. He spoke aloud in his thick, Jamaican-Brooklyn–bred accent:

> My Warrior Life Brothas and Sista Soljas
> The day of the Warrior Life Illuminati has begun
> This time, rather than the elites of the world sitting around
> > holding court
> It's you, the descendants of Pac, the remnants of the old
> > world order
> That lies at our feet begging, like those of you they once
> > spit on
> This is your turn, your time to reign
> To release yourselves from their chains

To make them slaves in your mines, to topple their corrupt
    rule
From the Congo to the jungles of Los Angeles
the Caribbean to the deserts in the Sudan and Iraq
G-Money spilled his blood on that very sand to start this
    revolution
It's time for you to take up the movement
The next generation of Warrior Life; you are the future
The past is mummified and you're newly come to life
Look to G-Money and this scripture whenever you need
    guidance
And know God-Money, his humble highness
Has your back; with one push of a button
I can reduce these bitches to nothin'
Warrior Life takin' over for the 2020
You have the power now!

G-Money was proud. He'd reached the conclusion of ten years of work
with this moment, a lifetime for anyone else who had more time on their
hands. G-Money had none to waste. With every second he'd had of freedom,
he'd lived a lifetime, created new life, not just a family but a tribe, seventy-
one children and counting, future leaders of the Warrior Life movement.
He had mirrored Pac's mindset from the moment he'd been released from
prison, and over the next and final eight months of his life, he'd recorded
over 150 songs and created the catalog and roots for a new generation to not
only bloom but grow for decades to come. His children would have children,
and their children would have children, and on it would go for ages, but this
was, no doubt, the age of God-Money.

He laughed as he watched on satellite while his Warrior Life stealth
crew of the world's best stone carvers chiseled away, adding a fifth face to
Mount Rushmore, that of G-Money. It was finally revealed to the world but
only in stone and painting. He would have much rather remained the man in
black, just like his homie Johnny Cash, another outlaw who sat on his wall,
playing cards with Pac, G-Money, and Elvis in a re-creation of the famed
Boulevard of Broken Dreams painting by Gottlieb Helnwein, where Elvis,
Humphrey Bogart, James Dean, and Marilyn Monroe hold court. He'd

commissioned the artist privately to paint it for him, and here it hung, next to priceless works by Picasso and Warhol, as well as a healthy collection of art by the world's leading African painters, from Congo-born Cheri Samba to Nigerian-bred Peju Alatise, revered contemporary Ivory Coast artist Aboudia Abdoulaye Diarrassouba, South Africa's Lionel Smit, and other artists from around the globe, like Mark Bradford, Ai Weiwei, Lubaina Himid, Wolfgang Tillmans, Njideka Akunyili Crosby, Pope.L, Yayoi Kusama, Haroon Mirza, Anne Imhof, Damien Hirst, Mika Rottenberg, Trevor Paglen, Laura Owens, David Hockney, and Cindy Sherman, all of whom had been commissioned to render portraits of G-Money's likeness, as it was revealed to the world for the first time with the release of the *Warrior Life Illuminati* doctrine.

He'd already had a lifetime of influence and was busy playing catch-up, working himself into the modern museum of contemporary and future historic pop and political culture, hanging both in gallery halls and on the walls of abandoned buildings in hoods around the world. For that creative endeavor, he'd hired the world's most wanted—and top-rated— graffiti artists, including the likes of Lee Quiñones, Blu, REAS, Revok, Seen UA, DAIM, Eduardo Kobra, Seak, Shepard Fairey—who'd done a world-famous likeness of former president Barack Obama (G-Money was most excited to see what Fairey would do with his likeness)—Sabo, Vhils, Invader, ESPO, Blek le Rat, OSGEMEOS, Dondi White, Lady Pink, KET, David Choe, RETNA, Laser 3.14, and many more. All had proudly signed up, some already staying free in the world to create under the protection of Warrior Life as they took to the streets with an army of artists to express themselves without fear of retribution, as they had only a few years before. Warrior Life was a symbol of that freedom that was already the most popular tag for up-and-coming graffiti artists everywhere, and G-Money had set it all in motion by setting them free.

Like Pac's rose growing out of concrete, the likeness of the Warrior Life leader around the world was protected, like the Mona Lisa. Along with being guarded by armed WL soljas outside of every building, as with the world's top art museums, from the Louvre in France to the Cenacolo Vinciano in Milan, the Galleria degli Uffizi and Gallerie dell'Accademia, Florence (the latter of which held Michelangelo's world-famous *David*), and of course the Musei Capitolini, where ancient Roman ruins were held.

G-Money was a Roman in his own time and proud to be displayed among the renderings of Roman emperors like Augustus, Trajan, Hadrian, Marcus Aurelius, and Aurelian, along with other great portraits of great world conquerors, like Julius Caesar and Napoleon, except G-Money would be celebrated in centuries to come as one of the world's great liberators. He had every great cultural epicenter covered, from the Rijksmuseum in Amsterdam to the Museo Nacional del Prado in Madrid, and on and on. He had even broken new ground by landing wall space at the Museum of Qin Terra-cotta Warriors and Horses in Xi'an, China; the Nezu Museum, the Miho Museum, and National Museum of Western Art in Tokyo, Japan; and even the International Friendship Exhibition in Hyangsan and the Victorious Fatherland Liberation War Museum in Pyongyang, North Korea; and the State Hermitage Museum in Russia.

Desperate to catch up with the hip factor of Western culture, G-Money had even penetrated the Middle East, from the Museum of Islamic Art in Doha, Qatar, to the Gezira Center for Modern Art and the Museum of Islamic Art in Cairo, Egypt; the Palestinian Museum in Birzeit, Palestine; the Sharjah Art Museum in Sharjah, United Arab Emirates; the Turkish and Islamic Arts Museum in Istanbul, Turkey; the Israel Museum in Jerusalem; the Tel Aviv Museum of Art; the Nalia Art Gallery; the National Museum of Riyadh, the Beautiful Names of Allah Gallery in Medina, the Al Tayebat International City in Jeddah, and Darat Safeya Binzagr, all in Saudi Arabia; and even the Tehran Museum of Contemporary Art in Tehran, Iran.

Last but not least, G-Money had made a private donation exclusively to the National Gallery in Washington, DC, of an entire collection of priceless paintings stolen by the Nazis in World War II—which he had reacquired, in its entirety, on the black market—in exchange for the gallery hanging a single portrait of his likeness. As a sign of his cutting-edge cultural relevance, despite the political pressure from their respective governments not to do so, all had privately negotiated for first-edition G-Money portraits by the world's top painters across the stylistic spectrum. Along with his face on the WL currency, this was to be the greatest unveiling the world would see since Michelangelo painted the Sistine Chapel. This was a new Renaissance, and G-Money wanted it captured vividly in living color.

He was, after all, the cultural ambassador to Warrior Life and its curator, along with its political and spiritual leader. Art had opened his eyes and ears for the first time, and he knew it would do so for the rest of the world too, as well as capture WL history as it was made. Ground had already been broken on Warrior Life's official museum in Jamaica's capital of Kingston, along with satellite wings around the globe and in struggling museums across Africa that desperately needed new funding. Now, he had devoted Warrior Life Movement wings, newly built or renovated, courtesy of generous multimillion-dollar endowments, to the Iziko Museums of South Africa; the Museum of Modern Art of Algiers, Algeria; the historic Red Castle Museum in Tripoli, Libya; the National Museum of Ethiopia; the Nairobi National Museum in Kenya; and the House of Slaves in Dakar, Senegal, all of which G-Money would turn into some of the most visited museums around the globe. His third-market strategy was as sound as any speculator who had bought up barren desert, knowing that, one day, he would strike oil. As usual, G-Money had invested in the third world, and he was already being publicly recognized as one of its greatest benefactors. He developed schools and pools where they'd never been before, and police forces, which were no longer corrupt or preying on the local populations, were instead kept on G-Money's payroll and making much more money each week as a result.

The crime rates in ghettos around the globe had plummeted because of Warrior Life's stronghold on the drug trades in their respective territories, bringing children out on the streets, playing again, where they'd previously feared catching a stray bullet from gang-related violence.

G-Money had ended the horrors of sex trafficking for millions of women around the same third world that he ruled now, and he planted the seeds for his power to grow and grow in the new age to come across societies around the world. The Warrior Life Illuminati had begun.

Printed in the United States
by Baker & Taylor Publisher Services